Angels Flight

BY CHRIS MEINTJES

Order this book online at www.trafford.com
or email orders@trafford.com

Most Trafford titles are also available at major online book retailers.

Note for Librarians: A cataloguing record for this book is available from Library
and Archives Canada at www.collectionscanada.ca/amicus/index-e.html

Printed in Victoria, BC, Canada.

ISBN: 978-1-4269-0842-2 (sc)
ISBN: 978-1-4269-0843-9 (dj)

Cover painting by Sandy Moffat
Edited by Michelle Willmers

*Our mission is to efficiently provide the world's finest, most comprehensive book publishing
service, enabling every author to experience success. To find out how to publish your book, your
way, and have it available worldwide, visit us online at www.trafford.com*

Trafford rev. 9/4/2009

 www.trafford.com

North America & international
toll-free: 1 888 232 4444 (USA & Canada)
phone: 250 383 6864 ♦ fax: 812 355 4082

Author Bio

C HRIS MEINTJES was born in South Africa and has a great love for the great wild spirit that Africa has in abundance. Chris has spent a great deal of time in the wild experiencing big skies and the great diversity of life that exists in the great savannahs and bush veldt.

Chris has had a love affair with Africa, its wildlife and its people for his entire life.

With the growing pressures of overpopulation and consumption economies, many parts of the African continent were finding themselves under pressure. With this in mind, Chris liked the idea of environmental heroes that found a way to conserve, protect and share the wild magic of Africa

Chris lives with his wife Shelley and his two children Sam and Maggie in Cape Town, South Africa and dreams of a better world

Acknowledgements

I WOULD LIKE to thank the love of my life, Shelley, for her love and support throughout our journey together. Also, to my children, you really are my greatest adventure.

I dedicate this, my first attempt at writing, to my family, Shelley, Sam and Maggie

Chapter 1
THE HERD

'Mopapi' nickname for an elephant
with angels wing ears - Mopapi Ngirozi

**05h45, Wednesday 12 September – Dawn in Africa in
a valley in the Chikangawa private reserve, Zimbabwe**

THE TALL riverine grass bowed to the light early morning
spring breeze as the day dawned. A dim, grey light was
growing on the horizon and a thick morning mist hung
low in the valley, whisping up the sides of the valley walls.
Tombstone-like tree trunks and boulders jutted from the mist
and caught the first greyness of dawn. The crackle of frogs in
and around the river filled the air. Down on the valley floor,
in amongst the large green Acacia trees, grey shadows stirred.
From amongst these shadows, ancient rumbles echoed, filling
the valley with a timelessness.

One of the shadows broke from the mist. Her grey wrinkled
skin glistened with dew and droplets of water had gathered
under her tusks. She turned her head to look across the valley
towards the crimson sky.

There she stood. At first completely still, then turning her
head to look across the valley. From deep inside her a droning
sound grew, an ageless echo of generations of her kind. The

deep call, low in tone, carried across the open valley and was once again answered by others standing amongst the trees. The rustling sound of eating emerged from the thicket. In the distance a nightjar whistled the dawn and the morning calls of birds started to softly overwhelm the dying sounds of night.

She flapped her unusually long ears and gave out one more haunting call before walking out slowly from the reeds onto the dry riverbank. Around her, in the mists and shadows of the trees, were all the members of her herd, some descended from her, and many others from other families, sharing the bounty of everything the valley had to offer. This was a good place with enough food and water for all.

She made her way slowly down to the water's edge, where two yearlings were playing in the water. Extending her trunk, she greeted each one by touching their heads and faces. They returned her greeting by touching her long trunk with theirs. There was gentleness and affection in this daily greeting. In this family everyone had their place and together they were able to prosper in this wild and beautiful place.

Behind her some of the older cows walked down to the water and, before taking a drink, greeted their matriarch affectionately. Throughout the whole herd, these interactions were taking place, entrenching the familial bonds of Africa's largest elephant herd. It was a ritual that had been played out for centuries by the ancestors of this great herd.

Rumblings poured from the different clustered groups, who, each in their own way, were starting the new day.

The matriarch then gave a long, deep droning call and turned towards the reeds on the other side of the river. The two yearlings tried to follow, but the bank on the opposite side was steep and they took turns falling back into the water. The matriarch turned and with gentle strength placed the end of her long, thick trunk on their backs, steadying them as they climbed the bank. Once they were up safely, she turned and wandered up into the reeds to start the morning feed.

The herd around her had rested well in the night and they were intent on feeding on the sweet young grasses close to the river's edge. The river was wide and had flourishing clumps of shrubs, grasses and thick trees, all thriving on the energy of the African sun and the rare abundance of water in this dry savannah land. Small, unopened flowers covered the open grassland and the early rains had caused seeds to start sprouting. She had seen this many times and knew that there would be good spring eating. She gave out another deep rumble of contentment and shook her large head slowly from side to side.

As the mist slowly lifted the breeze intensified and the sun warmed the air. Hundreds of bodies now emerged from the rising mist. Even with so many in number, they looked at peace with themselves and their surroundings.

Downwind from the herd, about a half a mile away, in the thick tree line, there was another cluster of shadows, also moving. These were cast by a small band of men, slowly moving closer to the herd. They stooped low under the cover of the thick clumps of riverside shrub and grass. The leader signalled them to stop and he pulled from his shoulder a large pair of binoculars. He scanned the herd until he had the matriarch in his sites and then signalled for them to move on again. This was repeated as they drew closer to the herd.

Unaware of the threat, the large elephant was now enjoying the sweet, crisp leaves that grew on the trees closest to the river. She used her trunk to carefully strip off the leaves and the ends of the branches that were the juiciest. Around her the herd was feeding and upriver some of the younger calves were taking a morning drink from a rock pool.

The band of men continued to draw closer until they reached a small clearing. Their leader carried a thirty odd six rifle, typical of the style used for hunting in these parts. This one was custom made, making it what many hunters called an 'elephant gun'. The hunter turned to the two men behind him.

'Quiet! We need to be quiet!' They both looked white eyed at their leader and stopped talking immediately. One of the men was very short, and he had a scar on each cheek, The other man was very thin but much younger than the others.

'These are the ones,' the leader whispered, pointing to the herd that was no more than two hundred yards from them. They were slightly hidden in the mist, but it was lifting fast.

'Don't let them see you. These are wild ones. I have heard stories told that their matriarch attacks first, no mock charges,' he whispered to the twosome jokingly. Elephants usually scare off threats by charging at them, but only a few carry out the charge to its conclusion. It was however legend that this herd was protected by the fiercest of matriarchs. The men cowered behind the camouflage of the thick foliage and the rising morning mist, frozen in the place they stood watching from.

The short man leaned towards the leader. 'Jonas, that one is the legend, is she not? I have heard about her. The one with the great spirit, the one that many local chiefs talk about. Look at her ears.'

Jonas answered. 'Yes, she is Mopapi, the one whose ears look like the wings of an angel.'

'Look at those tusks… they must be worth over a million.'

'Yes, but she is not an easy victim. Do you want to try?' Jonas joked with his companion, handing him his big elephant gun in a mocking gesture. The man shook his head and backed off.

'Not very brave, are we?' Jonas laughed quietly

'Big ears and big tusks, both bigger than usual for a female,' commented the young man.

'Do we call this in Jonas?' he asked.

'No, not yet. I want to get a little closer to her. I want to get a closer look at those tusks.'

'What if she sees you, boss?' the short man rubbed his head.

'If she sees me, I recommend you run. She will kill the slowest of us.' He turned to glance at the two men squatting behind him, their eyes now wide with fear as they gaped nervously across the open ground to Mopapi. Elephants were to be feared – especially this one, who had become legend. They had heard stories about her size, but none of them had caught a glimpse of her before; let alone gotten so close that they could see the creases in the skin of one of the largest female elephants on the continent.

'Not a sound. I am going to move across to the other side of this opening. Don't move a muscle before the fog blows in.'

Jonas and his two companions were poachers, highly trained in tracking large game and experts at quickly removing valued skins, tusks and horns. Jonas had worked in this reserve as a tracker for a year now. It had been a good cover to follow the herd, which, being the largest in Africa, would bring top dollar for their ivory. In fact, if the entire herd was killed, it would make for the biggest ivory delivery in history. The Colonel knew this and that was why Jonas was there. He and his team had done this for years. Working for reserves and parks in Zimbabwe and Zambia where they and others could profit from poaching. Today was no different.

Jonas signalled that he was going to move across the clearing and step-by-step, careful not to break any sticks that would alert the herd, he covered the ground to the other side where he crouched low under a fallen trunk and set up the scope on his rifle.

Mopapi had moved into the brush and was stripping off some of the tasty bark on a camelthorn tree. The yearlings were close behind, still crunching in the reeds.

Jonas signalled for the others to cross as Mopapi and the herd, still upwind, were in the cover of the tree line and reeds. The two crept across the clearing to where Jonas was squatting, looking into the telescopic sight of his rifle.

'She is a big one, and the one who kills her will be revered as a great hunter.' Jonas pulled away from the scope and looked at his companions.

'Do you think we should get ourselves a bonus?' Jonas looked at his companions with a broad, white-toothed smile.

'What do you mean, boss?'

'Why don't we take this one for ourselves? We can take her down, get the truck in and by midday we could be at Rundu station, a million dollars richer?'

'But what if we get caught, boss? We are supposed to be scouting for the Colonel.'

Maybe we can do this for ourselves. He will never know and I have the right people to trade with. If his operation fails at least we will have money to show for it.'

'But boss, we haven't got the equipment.'

'We do. I have a long metal saw and a chainsaw in the truck. It will do. We have enough fuel in the truck to drive to Rundu. What else do we need?'

The others started to contemplate the situation. The money would be good, and they could probably still help with the bigger operation and get paid for that too.

They reached agreement, and Jonas smiled at the prospect of being rich again. Too many years working for others had left him bitter with those he had always worked for. He had seen many from his home get rich but he had been left to look after an exploited family who would never find their way out of debt and poverty.

'No more money for those fat cats, those politicians that talk and talk and then steal from those they have made promises to. The time for us is now, it's here on a plate for us,' Jonas whispered under his breath and looked back to see his prize. Mopapi was there, in his reach. He would be a legend and he would be rich. The thought of success made his mouth water. His heart was beating faster and he could feel the excitement of the hunt inside him.

Lining up his rifle, he moved into position, flat on his stomach with the barrel of the gun extended beneath the trunk. The other two men lay next to him. Through the scope he could see Mopapi moving around between the camelthorn trees. He needed a shot to the head or to the heart. A head shot would bring Mopapi down, but only if it was through the temple. A shot to the heart was easier, as the area of softer tissue around the front of the chest made a larger target. Jonas wriggled into a more stable and comfortable position, legs wide apart for stability and his body flat, making the shot as stable as possible. He could see Mopapi more clearly now through the scope. The crosshairs were aimed at her shoulder, but the two yearlings were on a small ridge between where he was and where Mopapi was feeding. He waited. Mopapi, still behind the trees, turned and walked out into the open. Jonas tightened his grip and moved his finger into trigger position. He needed to make this shot and it needed to be clean. The herd would disperse in panic if their matriarch were to go down.

Mopapi, oblivious to Jonas, was making her way directly towards him and was now no more than a hundred yards away. Jonas could feel the adrenaline pumping, its effect steadying his arms and shoulders. He lined up for the shot. He pulled his finger back and a shot rang out, thundering across the valley. Every animal across the valley froze. Mopapi looked in the direction of the thundering sound, and could see movement below a large ironwood tree trunk. She began to rage, but then felt the pain in her left shoulder. Without pause, she charged. At first she did not know what it was she should be chasing, but she ran towards the sound of the rifle shot and after a few paces saw through blurred vision the shape she had come to associate with fear and pain, the outline of a kneeling man. She had heard this sound before and each time one of her family had died. She wanted to stop it from ever happening again.

Jonas reloaded as quickly as he could, realising that he must have missed the shot as Mopapi showed no sign of being hit at all. Every time he had fired the rifle at an animal before, his target had fallen.

'How could I have missed? She was right in the middle of my sights, an easy shot!' He gritted his teeth and brought the rifle up to his shoulder again. Mopapi was covering the ground quickly. He would only have one more chance.

He pulled the trigger again, but still she came. Jonas was starting to panic. Mopapi was now only yards away from the trunk he sheltered behind, and Jonas turned to see his companions running up to the ridge where there were some rocks large enough to protect them from a raging elephant. He leapt to his feet, but it was too late. Mopapi was on him, pushing aside the large fallen tree with ease. Jonas made only a few steps before trunk and tusk slammed into him. He was knocked to the ground, screaming, his rifle tossed to the side like a small twig. He realised that after all these years his arrogance had finished him. The reality filled him with fear. He knew it was over for him and his eyes were wide with terror and panic.

Mopapi ploughed into him, trumpeting loudly, ears flapping. She trampled him repeatedly, and then, turning on her heels, ran back fifty yards toward the herd and turned again to look at this faceless enemy.

The herd had run some distance away from the shots, but had stopped. All those who were in sight of their matriarch were looking intently at her for a signal. They too were afraid, but she had not run; instead choosing to confront the threat. They waited, ears flapping, looking back to where the shots had come from. Mopapi was filled with rage as she remembered others falling to the hunter's gun. She stood there, looking through blurred eyes at the body that lay in the sand, motionless. Her chest heaved, taking in deep breaths, and the tip of her trunk sent up puffs of dust every time she exhaled. Her shoulder burnt with pain. On the left side of her chest, just in front of her shoulder, there were two red holes, both oozing bright red blood, which ran slowly down her chest and onto her leg. But the bleeding was not heavy. The place where the bullets had hit was protected by hard bone. The pain would be hard to bear, but the shots had not been fatal.

Jonas lay motionless in the settling dust. His back was broken and a tusk had sliced his left arm to the bone, leaving a splattering of red blood and torn flesh. His mind was racing with shock. It all seemed like a dream and above him the mist was clearing to a glorious blue sky. He tried to turn his head, but could not. The fact that he could feel nothing made him think that he was still fine, just winded. With every effort he tried to move his arm to wipe the dust from his eyes, but he could not. He tried again, thinking maybe his hands were stuck, but he failed to move at all. His eyes flickered around, looking for his companions, but there was no sign of them. He tried to shout, but only a short breath of air passed his lips. His eyes were watering from the dust. His lip quivered as he started to take in what had happened to him.

Jonas's companions looked down from the rocks, wide-eyed, shaking. Neither of them dared to go down to him for fear that they would share his fate. They could see him lying twisted in the clearing. They had been running away when Mopapi had caught him, so did not see him fall.

'Is he alive?'

'He's not moving.'

'Jonas! Jonas!' one of them shouted. 'Are you alright?'

There was no answer.

Mopapi heard the shouts, and rage once again welled up inside her. She charged for a second time, racing towards Jonas and the sounds from the rocks above him. She kicked up dust while she ran. Shaking her head and waving her trunk, she heard a call from the herd. The yearlings were following her. She was drawn away from her rage and immediately instinct told her to protect the young ones and move the herd away from this place. The pain in her shoulder had worsened and she could feel the wet stickiness of blood. She could also smell it; reminding her of the deaths she had experienced in years gone by. She looked up towards the rocks, but saw no movement. She gave one last look to Jonas, who had not moved in her second charge, and gave out a loud trumpet call before turning towards the herd. At speed she signalled to the herd to run and gathered up the yearlings before moving off down the valley, the herd running ahead of her. Every hundred yards or so, Mopapi would turn around and stop, looking back to see if anything was following them. Nothing did. Only the clouds of dust that slowly drifted off in the morning breeze.

As the sun's first rays hit the valley floor, the herd had almost disappeared from sight and stillness fell on the valley again.

The two men stayed in the trees as the herd retreated.

'Shall we go and see him?'

'She might come back.'

They were shaking with fear. They had never seen such rage in an elephant before.

'We had better go down and see.'

Very carefully, the two men crept towards the hunter, their loaded rifles ready. Jonas lay completely still. He had closed his eyes to shelter them from the dust.

'Jonas!' both men had arrived and knelt at his side. 'Are you alright?' Jonas looked mauled, but maybe it wasn't that bad. Maybe they had all been lucky.

'I am not sure. I can't feel anything. I can't move.'

Jonas's arm was bleeding badly. The two men tried to stop the bleeding by tearing pieces of cloth from their shirts, and making a tourniquet. It did not seem to help.

'We must get help, Jonas.'

'Yes, go. Get the truck and come back for me. Hurry up.'

The two men looked at each other, still in a state of shock and panic.

'One of us must stay.'

Jonas looked up, but his eyes were glazed.

'You are faster then me' said the short man. 'I will go' and the young man stood, looked down at Jonas and then turned and ran back into the bush.

Chapter 2
SALLY DISCOVERS THE PLOT

'Chikangawa': a game reserve and a place of haven and safety

07h00, Wednesday 12 September –
Over the ridge from the Tlokwe valley

'DID YOU hear something?' Sally Allenby turned to her assistant and long-time companion, Thabo Mhlungu. She was sitting on a fold-up stool, her long blonde hair blowing across her freckled face. She stood and pulled her hair back, showing intelligent ice-blue eyes.

'Sounded like gun shots' Thabo answered, looking up to the ridge that rose up next to them. Thabo was over six foot tall and had broad shoulders. He was wearing reserve khakis and a name tag on his pocket that read 'Head Game Ranger'. A strong, muscular man, he had been raised in the bush and at the age of thirty-seven had seen more action in his conservation duty than some soldiers do in warfare. He was a proud man, with a big heart.

'Sounded like it was coming from over the ridge in the valley and it did not sound like a normal shot. It sounded like a high calibre.' Sally listened carefully. Another shot followed.

'Damn it, that doesn't sound good.' Thabo threw down the clipboard he was working on. 'The big herd is up there, I am sure of it.'

Sally looked across at Thabo. 'Poachers?' There was dread on her face.

'Yes. We had better get down there.'

Sally tossed aside the paperwork they had been filling out for the day and followed Thabo as they rushed to the Land Rover. He started the engine and revved it loudly as they drove off, kicking up dust behind the tyres as they spun in the dry sand.

'Damn it, I forgot to pack away the vaccine packs, they are going to spoil.' cursed Sally.

'You want to go back?' asked Thabo as he tore up the side of the ridge along a flat rock formation.

'Its fine. I have more back at camp, but those lions need them sooner rather than later.'

Sally's head and body were being bounced back and forth by the rough terrain. The two of them had been camping out, following a pride of lion that were suffering from a tuberculosis outbreak. They were administering inoculations with coloured darts, leaving small ink stains on the pride members so that they could keep track of the pride members and the dosage when they re-injected them next spring.

Sally, a slim, round-faced thirty-six-year-old was the Chikangawa veterinarian and also one of the reserve's trustees. Thabo was not just the head game ranger, but also one of Sally's closest friends. His father was the chief of the area, a man everyone respected for his wisdom, honesty and traditional values. Thabo was the same way and he and Sally made a very good team. They had grown this reserve into one of the most successful in Africa, with a balanced ecosystem and good breeding projects for other less successful reserves, especially for wild dog and cheetah. They were also widely respected by the conservation community for being people who put into action what many others just talked about.

Thabo drove the Land Rover off the flat rocks and followed some narrow sand tracks that the antelope used to go down to the water in the valley beyond. They listened for any more shots over the drone of the engine, but heard nothing. As they approached the summit of the ridge, Sally picked up the radio and changing the frequency, radioed Marcus Stein, the head ranger and manager of the anti-poaching unit at the main tourist camp of Chikangawa.

'Marcus, come in. It's Sally.'

The radio hissed static back at her.

'Marcus, can you read?'

The radio crackled and the throaty voice of Marcus appeared.

'Sally, good morning, you're on the horn early. Beautiful day?'

'Yes Marcus, we may have a problem. Thabo and I are at the edge of Tlokwe valley, about six miles up on the western side. We heard some gun shots from the valley. Please advise of any activity your team may have in the area.'

'None at all, Sally, the team are all here at camp.'

'Okay. This doesn't sound good. We're going to take a look. Are there any armed personnel near us?'

'I don't know, Sally. Let me get back to you. Be careful.' Marcus signed off.

Thabo negotiated some rocks and the wheels of the Land Rover started to slip. He shifted the Landrover into low range four-wheel drive, and revving the engine, shoved the vehicle into second gear and found traction. Guiding the vehicle through the rocks, they started to move slowly over the rim of the valley wall.

'Take it slow at the top, we don't want to alarm anyone,' Sally warned.

Thabo smiled and drove the final fifty yards to the rim, where he slowly guided the Land Rover to a stop. They both jumped from the vehicle and crouched as low as possible, moving to the edge so that they could see the valley and the river below.

Sally passed Thabo her binoculars. She had contact lenses and they always seemed to blur. He lay down on a flat rock and steadied himself before scanning the riverbed below for movement. Sally saw the herd first, moving north quite fast, leaving a trail of swirling dust. They were most probably about two miles away.

'Something's not right,' said Thabo, looking through the binoculars, 'they are running away, but from what I cannot see. If we heard right, we may have some poachers on our hands.'

'I'll radio Marcus again.'

Sally moved back to the Land Rover and grabbed the handset

'Marcus, come in, Sally.'

'Yes Sal, I am here. See anything yet?'

'Yes, the big herd of tuskers is fleeing from something in the valley. But we're not sure from what. Those shots were not from any of ours, please alert the guys, not sure how soon you can get here. Is the chopper available? Can you send someone immediately? I want to catch these bastards.'

'We don't have anyone close to you, but we have called the airfield and the chopper is being prepped. Should be in the air in twenty minutes or so.'

'If they flee, they'll go north. There are a lot of places for them to disappear in up there, especially if they go into the villages at the gate. Send someone up there to keep an eye out.'

Sally could see Thabo flattening himself on the rock to get more stability.

'I have to go. Hurry, Marcus.'

'Will do, Sal. Keep safe and do not take any unnecessary risks. We are more than an hour away, so don't get too close – identify and follow, but don't engage, that is our job.'

'Will try, what channel you guys on?'

'We will stay on five, keep me updated. We are on our way.'

Sally signed off, and opened the back of the Land Rover to take out the two air rifles and a box of drug darts they had been using on the smaller pride members while doing their check-ups. Unfortunately all they had was a half pack of air darts that they had been using for immunisation.

Sally rejoined Thabo at the vantage point where he was still looking through the binoculars at the terrain below.

'Anything yet, Baphu?' asked Sally, using Thabo's nickname.

'Not yet, no movement.'

Thabo worked back from where the elephant were still running, keeping an eye on the clumps of bush scattered around the river below. And then he spotted movement.

'I have something, down there.' Thabo pointed at a clump of thick shrub bush surrounded by some tall acacia trees and old dead tree trunks, it was about half a mile away.

Sally could not see what it was, but it was moving.

'Can you see them?' asked Sally.

'Yes, they are coming out of the brush … two of them. Strange!' Thabo looked up from the binoculars.

'What's strange?'

'They are moving very carefully, I can't see them very well but they seem to be crouching behind that old trunk.' Thabo pointed to the big trunk that lay out in the open and passed Sally the binoculars.

'I can't see them. We should move down to get a better look. Did you see if they were armed?'

'Yes I think so. I couldn't see clearly, but they looked like they were carrying rifles. Hold on, there is a truck down there too, parked off behind those trees. They must have driven it down the side of the river, there is no track from the south.'

'Bloody bastard Poachers. What do we do now?' Sally looked at Thabo, relying on his experience.

'We have a choice, stay here and keep an eye on them – or tackle them with what we've got.'

Thabo and Sally looked at each other again and with a flash in his eye, Thabo nodded his head. Sally nodded in reply and they stood up and loaded each rifle with a single dart.

'Not much firepower,' Sally smiled.

They started to move down into the valley, following a narrow antelope trail between the thorn bushes and aloes.

A hundred yards down, the path opened out into rocky outcrops and on top of one of these they had a clear view of the river below. Crawling to the edge, Thabo took another look at the men below.

'Can you see anything?' asked Sally

'Yes, I have them. There are three, one is lying down, the others are crouching next to him, their backs are to us. Maybe we can move down between the rocks and get closer without being seen.'

Sally looked concerned. 'Shouldn't we wait for backup?'

'Even if they had the chopper close by, they would take at least an hour to get here. These guys will be long gone. They have their backs to us at the moment. We can creep down into that crag and with two shots we might be able to immobilise two of them. Be very quiet.'

'I am with you.' Sally touched Thabo on the shoulder and he understood that he was to lead them into this dangerous situation.

Thabo had worked in conservation for the last decade and he had seen it all – poachers, corrupt officials, drunken hunters and epidemics. Sally had only worked with Thabo for a few years, but together they made a formidable pair, nurturing the reserve as well as managing the sensitive balance between herbivore and carnivore.

They made their way down the smooth, grey rocks which led them out onto a small flat overhang only sixty meters from the men. On their bellies, rifles loaded and close to hand, Thabo took another look.

'They are definitely poachers, looks like ivory or horn. All of them are carrying high-calibre rifles. The one on the ground is not moving, but seems to be speaking to the others. He looks injured. We are close enough for a shot.' Thabo looked to Sally for a final decision.

'Yes, lets do it. This might be our only chance, and I think we have a pretty clear shot from here. I'll take the one with the khaki hat, you can take the other one.' Thabo nodded.

'What is the load?' Thabo asked, referring to the dosage in the darts they were using.

'Enough to take them down for an hour or so. Give them two or three minutes before they go down.'

They both brought the rifles forward and, splaying their legs, they locked the two men into their sights. Sally looked through a simple sight, clear for moving targets with a large red star in the middle. She was comfortable with her rifle and she had been using it for many years. She knew Thabo was one of the finest shots. He had an older rifle with a wider scope. The scope made it easier to follow a target, but more difficult to hit one.

'On my mark.' Thabo slipped his finger round the trigger. Sally did the same, both pulling back slightly so that they could feel the trigger pushing back, just short of firing. The rifles, being older, did not need much more pull to let the hammer go.

'Three, two, one.' Two shots rang across the bushveld.

The two men, startled by the shots and the sudden, sharp pain in their shoulders, turned to look up the ravine. A bright red coloured dart was imbedded in each of them. They pulled out the darts, grabbed their rifles and ran into the cover of the surrounding trees. They then started to take shots into the ravine. The clatter of the shots was deafening.

'Who are you?' shouted the short man.

'What do you want?' shouted the other.

The firing stopped. Both men were feeling the effects quickly. They had been perspiring and their heart rates were already high from Mopapi's attack. Anaesthetic now pumped through their veins..

Sally and Thabo kept their heads down low, away from the shots, but Thabo thought that they may have been seen. He was right. One of the men looked out from the side of a tree trunk and pointed in their direction.

'Lets hope that the dosage is sufficient.' He looked across at Sally, moving slightly to obscure her from the men's view.

'It will be, it's enough for a small antelope,' she shouted back, no longer concerned as the sound of gunfire disappeared and the shouting stopped.

It took no more than a few minutes for the anaesthetic to kick in, and the two men slowly dropped down into the sand.

'Nice shooting, Sal.' Thabo smiled at her.

'Good practice dealing with the lions,' she smiled back as she climbed down off the shelf of rock.

The two made their way slowly down to the fallen trunk and the man lying motionless in front of it. As they approached, Thabo turned to Sally, looking surprised.

'Jonas. Its Jonas!'

Jonas, could see the two of them approaching and his eyes welled up with tears. Thabo knelt down and looked at the man whose damaged limbs were beyond repair.

'Jonas, what are you doing here?'

Jonas was Thabo's cousin, his uncle's first-born, and they came from the same village on the outskirts of Chikangawa. Thabo was shocked and confused to see him here.

Jonas looked up through his tears, mumbling. 'I can't move.'

'What are you doing here?' Thabo's surprise was now turning into anger, bewilderment.

'I cannot tell you, cousin.'

Sally knelt down and started going over Jonas's vitals, checking the wound to his arm.

'This is from an elephant. You can see the tracks and this gash on his arm must be from a tusk.'

Thabo touched the ground next to Jonas body, looking at the signs of dust and dirt for a picture of what had happened.

'Jonas, you must tell me what you were doing here.' Thabo moved his face close to Jonas.

Jonas looked away and shut his eyes.

Thabo slapped him hard on the face, anger at a family member being involved in this disgrace.

'Jonas, you will tell me what you have done here.' Thabo spoke in Shona, his mother tongue.

The words hurt Jonas more than the blow, and tears started to well up in his eyes. He turned his face. looking at Thabo he spoke in a whisper.

'I am sorry, Bhuthi. This thing I have done is not the first time. This thing that I have done, it is bigger than you. You will not be able to stop it. These ones, this herd that you protect. It is over for them, they will all be gone, he is coming.'

'Who is coming?' asked Thabo.

'Moroge, he wants the herd, he needs the herd. He is coming soon.'

Just then, Thabo and Sally heard the crackle of the radio and saw that the big hand-held that was lying next to Jonas was set to transmit, meaning that whoever was on the other end could hear what they were saying. Sally grabbed the radio and switched it to receive. All she heard was a bit of static and the click of the radio being turned off.

'Jonas, what is this? Who are you working for? Who is Moroge?' Thabo grabbed Jonas by his shirt.

'Careful, Thabo. Unless we get him help soon he is going to die.' Sally looked at Jonas, his eyes showed a man who knew that he was at the end of his road.

'Jonas, you are my father's brother's child, please tell me what you have done, I need to know. You grew up with me, we went through initiation together. If you tell us we may be able to stop something terrible that you have started here.'

'Bhuthi, there is nothing you can do. Moroge is a Colonel in the army, he is one of the old guard and he is coming for the ivory and there is nothing you can do to stop him.' Jonas shut his eyes from the glare of the sun and dropped his head back into the dirt.,Sally broke out her water bottle and carefully tipping the bottle gave him a drink.

'Tell me when this is to happen.' Thabo has a sense of urgency now in his questions.

'Now, soon.' Jonas began to choke and blood trickled from his mouth.

'How soon, Jonas? How soon?' Thabo's fist tightened on Jonas's shirt.

'They are on their way. That is why we are here, to spot where the herd is so that they can come straight here.' Blood gurgled in Jonas's throat and Sally helped Thabo roll him over so that he did not choke.

Sally looked at Thabo. 'What are we going to do, Thabo? Go to the authorities?'

'Sally, I know this colonel. He was part of the liberation army, a veteran, feared by his peers. He is a powerful man. What troubles me is that he is very connected. Going to the authorities is not going to help. They are in his pockets. They would rather betray their community than cross him. They have already started taking land from my people, even though we are black just like them. They seem to think they are royalty.'

Sally could see the anger in Thabo's eyes. He had never been a big supporter of this government, especially since the land grabs and the poverty had gotten so much worse. His people were suffering.

Thabo looked down at his cousin.

'You disappoint me. Jonas. You of all people should know about building not destroying. When is all this going to end?'

Jonas started to choke again and this time a lot of blood spewed from his mouth and nose.

'Jonas, who else is involved from this side?' Thabo pulled Jonas up so that their faces were just inches apart.

'Thabo, he is dying. Let him down.'

Sally put her hand on Thabo's, who in turn eased his grip and let Jonas slip back down onto the sand.

Jonas's body jerked up as more blood oozed from his mouth. With Thabo holding his shirt tightly in his fists, starring into his eyes, Jonas gave out his last breath and his eyes glazed over. Thabo used his sand-covered hand to close his cousin's eyes, pausing there before smashing his flat hand onto the ground.

'We must stop this. If Jonas is right the Colonel could already be here.' Sally could see that Jonas was overwhelmed with anger and emotion, and she took over as decision-maker.

'Sal, if we want to stop this man, we will need help and there is no-one in the government that will do it. Unless you have a lot of money that you can throw at it, I am not sure we can do anything.'

'Thabo, what about Tom? Tom Stone? You know him quite well.'

Thabo thought about it and smiled.

'Yes, that is a good idea; I am not too sure where he is though. You have any ideas?'

'I'm not sure, but the last time we spoke he was in London.'

'Yes, he is well connected, maybe he can help. Is he still involved?'

'I think so, The last time I saw him he was here but it was about two years ago. They visited the park and he was completely taken with the herd. I think that was when you were away.'

'We had better get hold of him. If the Colonel is here or close, Tom might be able to give us information on who can help us down here and fast.' Thabo stood up and walked away from Jonas.

'We need to speak to Marcus. He can get a team together.'

Sally pulled a GPS from her bag and noted the position where Jonas's body lay. Pulling out her radio she called Marcus and gave him the exact location.

'We are just behind the ridge. We'll be there in fifteen minutes.'

Chapter 3
THE COLONEL

COLONEL MOROGE sat at his desk looking out of his office window at the cloudless blue sky. His office was large and over-furnished with dark teak tables and chairs. A leather lounger sat in the corner of the room, draped in a large lion skin, and the colours of the office were maroons and browns. His desk, positioned at a right angle to the window, was cluttered with papers, his inbox overflowing with brown and yellow folders. His mind was elsewhere. The Colonel was the Military Assistant to the Minister of the Interior, a job he felt beneath him. Why should he, a veteran of the struggle, be required to support a man he did not respect?

There was a knock at the door.

'Enter.' The Colonel swivelled his chair back to his desk and waited for his visitor.

In walked an adjutant with the Colonel's morning tea and messages. He placed the tray on the corner of the desk and placed the Colonel's mail and messages into a silver box elaborately decorated with beads.

The Colonel picked up his messages immediately and read through them, ignoring the adjutant's salute. He had been waiting for something in particular.

The Colonel found what he was looking for; a message that simply read: 'Chikangawa off, too hot.'

It was from his second in command.

'Damn it.' The Colonel muttered under his breath as he picked up his telephone and dialled a number. It rang twice before someone answered.

'Hello!' cracked a voice on the other side.

'Mamabe please, it is Moroge.'

'Hold on sir, I will transfer you.'

The Colonel waited for a moment and then the deep voice of Mamabe answered.

'Hello, Sir.'

'Mamabe, what is with this note? What is going on?' the Colonel barked into the telephone.

'Sir, we are discovered. Jonas is dead, killed by one of the elephant, and the girl, the Chikangawa doctor, she spoke to Jonas. I heard the conversation on the radio. He must have left it on. She knows about the operation.'

'How did this happen, Mamabe? You were supposed to find the elephant, not get caught.'

'Sir, it was Jonas and his crew. They were greedy and decided to go after the big one, the one they call Mopapi.'

'What are you saying?' the Colonel sat up from his seat, and small beads of sweat oozed from his brow.

'Sir, I do not know. I thought Jonas was one of us, but he wanted the ivory for himself.'

'We go ahead as planned. But it must happen this week. I will leave tomorrow morning and will meet you at the rendezvous point at eighteen hundred. As usual if I want anything done properly, I have to do it myself.'

'Yes, Sir.' Mamabe replied as the Colonel slammed down the telephone.

The Colonel stood up from his chair, walked to the window and looked out at downtown Harare. In front of him, the

Zimbabwean flag was flapping in the morning breeze. It was a symbol of the fight for freedom that he had been a part of and it raised strong feelings in him.

He thought back to the old days when things seemed simple and it was clear who the enemy was. These days he seemed to be locked in a battle with everyone, and he increasingly trusted nobody. He pulled a small black leather wallet from his pocket and removed a photograph of three smiling faces – his wife, his daughter (who had a silky, dark skin and a wide, happy smile) and his granddaughter, who had the same pretty features as her mother.

'This is for you. I am doing this all for you.' he mumbled as he placed the photograph on his desk and opened a draw to pull out a folder. Opening the left flap, he pulled out a travel pouch, inside of which were four tickets from Johannesburg to London. The Colonel thought of a new life there and how he would be respected for the role he had played in his country's struggle, a leader in society.

He picked up the telephone and dialled a number, tipping his head to secure the handset on his shoulder while he ruffled through papers on his desk in frustration.

The phone seemed to ring forever before it was answered by a woman with a soft, warm voice.

'Bomama?' The Colonel's demeanour changed instantly as he greeted his wife.

'Ah, my husband. How are you today?'

He could hear sounds of his granddaughter shrieking playfully in the background.

'I am fine. How is my family doing?'

'We are all fine. Your granddaughter has started to walk. It was a very happy moment. When will you be coming home so that you can see her? She misses her grandfather.'

'Soon. Very soon. I have some urgent business I must attend to, but I will try and get home before the end of the week.'

'Good. Is everything alright, my dear?'

Moroge suddenly felt tired. Tired of the army and of this country and of never being able to get anywhere.

'I am fine. I just wanted to hear your voice. Tell my granddaughter I say hello.'

'I will. Do you want to speak to your daughter?'

'No, I must go, I will call you soon to let you know when I will be home.'

'Good, we will cook something special.'

The Colonel put down the receiver and sunk back into his chair as his mind wandered to the busy city of London where he had bought a small house. With the money from this operation they could live a good life and his granddaughter would be raised in a proper country; not one beset by war and greed. It would be difficult to say goodbye, but it would have to be done. His application for asylum would be accepted and his family would be safe. Even after all that he had done, the special police would not be able to get at him there.

The Colonel rose from his desk and walked to his window.

'I will miss my Zimbabwe,' he sighed. 'I have fought long and hard for you, but I cannot fight anymore.'

He walked to the phone and rang for his adjutant. A few moments later the door opened.

'Sir, you called?'

'Yes, I want you to take care of something for me. I need to get to the Chikangawa Reserve for some urgent business. Can you make the necessary arrangements for me to be flown to the nearest airport?'

'Yes, Sir. When would you like to leave?'

'Immediately.'

'Yes, Sir. Anything else?'

'Yes, call my wife and tell her that I have organised a surprise trip for her and my daughter and granddaughter. I want you to organise safe transport to the Harare Airport for our flights to Johannesburg.'

'Yes, Sir. Will you need me to organise those tickets, Sir?'

'Yes, but don't book them through my office. They are for my own personal use, so use the travel agent and make the trip unofficial.'

'Yes. Sir. When should I book them for?'

'Monday next week. We will need to be at the airport in Johannesburg by 6pm. It is of utmost importance that you get this right. My family's happiness depends on it.'

'Yes. Sir. Of course. Is there anything else?'

'Yes. Do not tell my wife where we are going. It must be a surprise. Tell them to pack for a week's holiday.'

'Yes, Sir.'

'That is all.' The Colonel waved the adjutant's dismissal.

After the door shut, the Colonel pulled out a small black diary. He looked for a number and dialled it on the telephone. After two rings, a voice answered hello.

'It is Moroge.'

'Yes, Colonel. How are you?'

'I am fine. I am phoning to confirm delivery of a shipment.'

'Good, Colonel. We are waiting.'

'We should have the shipment for you by Sunday night. But first I need to confirm immediate payment on delivery.'

'Yes, Colonel. As discussed, we will remunerate you fully once we receive the shipment.'

'What price are you going to give me?'

'The usual per kilogram. Are we confirmed for the bridge at the southern gate of Chikangawa?'

'Yes, I will call to confirm what time we will be there. It will be sometime after dark on Sunday.'

The phone clicked and went dead.

The Colonel replaced the receiver slowly and pulled a handkerchief from his pocket to wipe the drops of sweat from his forehead.

Chapter 4
TOM STONE

15h45, Wednesday 12 September – Chikangawa Main Camp

SALLY AND Thabo drove to the main camp at Chikangawa, about thirty kilometres east of the Tlokwe valley. They had driven in stony silence for the last hour of their drive back from the valley.

'I still can't believe Jonas was so bent.' Thabo was shaking his head, still in a daze, the reality of his cousin's death slowly dawning on him. He pulled up outside three round thatch buildings, which were the park offices.

'We need to move quickly. You said you have the number for Tom?' Sally's voice was shaky. She was upset about the herd, but she tried to focus on what had to be done next. The herd was Chikangawa, and that troop of elephants meant everything to her. If they went, she would have to go too and she wasn't ready for that. This was her family and she had made many sacrifices in the years she had been here. She climbed from the vehicle and headed towards the reception doors.

'Wait here, I'll go and get Tom's number. I hope we can reach him. If there's anybody who can help us now, it's Tom.' Thabo touched Sally's shoulder. 'Are you going to be okay?'

Tears welled up, but she fought them back.

'It may already be too late. Maybe we've lost this place and the government has already decided to take it over.'

'We will never let that happen. This place belongs to all of us and we will do whatever we need to do.'

'Yes, let's get Tom on the line.'

Sally entered the thatched offices and switched on her computer. Marcus and his team were out and the offices were empty. She was happy to be out of the heat, on her own, with a few moments to gather her thoughts.

Minutes later Thabo arrived back with a well-worn black notebook. He handed it to Sally with a page open. On it was a London number for Tom Stone. Sally got an open line and dialled the number on speaker phone. The phone rang three times before it was answered.

'Hello, Tom speaking.'

'Tom, this is Thabo Mhlungu from Chikangawa in Zimbabwe.'

'Thabo, how are you? It's been ages. Are you in London?'

'No, Tom. I am phoning you from the bush.'

'Well, to what do I owe this pleasure? Is everything okay out there?'

'No, Tom. We have a problem.' A crackle in Thabo's voice belied his anxiety.

'Hold on a second, let me close the door,' Tom answered. 'Ok, how can I help?'

'Tom, you remember Sally?'

'Yes, I do, Chikangawa's lovely vet?' Tom answered

'Yes, she's here with me,' answered Thabo.

'Hi, Tom.' Sally tried to sound cheery.

'Hi Sally. Are you guys alright?'

'Tom, we have a problem. We had a run-in with some poachers this morning and have discovered that our big elephant herd is the target of a colonel in the army who's after their ivory. Him and his men are likely to attack the herd this weekend and wipe them out completely.'

'The big herd? I thought the park was safe and that the local community were supporting you now?'

'Yes, that was the idea,' answered Sally, 'but it seems this colonel is a renegade. He's bad news, Tom. This could destroy the park.'

'What about the authorities?'

'No go, Tom,' answered Thabo. 'He is high up, untouchable. It would take weeks to get some sort of enquiry going and we don't have that long. We need to do something ourselves. Now.'

'Can you arrange for the herd to be moved at short notice?'

'We don't have the manpower and are pretty sure the colonel has spies everywhere. Do you know anyone that could help?'

'Yes, perhaps, but not at such short notice.'

'Please, Tom.' Sally's voice was desperate now and she was on the verge of tears.

'Okay, we'll work something out. Give me your number and I'll call you tomorrow. We're not going to lose this herd. I will do everything in my power to help. I mean it ... everything.' Tom's voice took on a stern determined tone.

'Thank you, Tom,' replied Thabo and Sally in chorus.

Thabo gave Tom the number and hung up.

'Do you think he can help us?' Sally looked pleadingly at Thabo.

'If there is anybody on this planet that can help us, it's Tom Stone. Everything is going to be okay, Sally. Tom is our man.'

'I hope so. What does Tom really do, Thabo?'

'He takes from those who damage our fragile environment and he gives to those who are fighting for it. Like Robin Hood, just a little more ruthless. Now we wait for his phone call.'

Sally stared blankly across the room.

'I will get us something to eat. We need to stay strong, Sally.'

Thabo walked out of the room, leaving Sally to her thoughts. She was sure that all was lost.

Chapter 5
THE JOB

09h30, Thursday 13 September – Southfield's, London

Tom Stone woke to the sound of traffic below his Southfield's flat. The call from Thabo and Sally had him working through the night. He had tried to sleep, but could only think of the large herd, now under threat. Things had been quiet for a while, but Thabo and Sally's phone call had shocked him into action and he felt alive with purpose.

Tom's flat was situated on the top floor of a renovated hundred-year-old three-storey in the heart of South London and as he looked out of his window he could see the flags above Wimbledon's centre court blowing in the morning breeze. Another grey day. Autumn was always like this. Stretching, he yawned and made his way down the passage to the kitchen. As Tom walked down the passage he knocked on one of the doors before going into the bathroom.

'I'm up, sleepy head. Its already ten,' a voice boomed from behind the closed door.

The flat was a large three-bedroom, with modern finishes throughout. The passageway was covered in paintings and photographs of wild animals and sunsets, which contrasted starkly with the stainless-steel kitchen and the grey carpets.

'I was up late. Our new project is taking shape. Did you sleep well, Pop?'

'For sure. Always do and always will.'

'Good, because we're going to have a busy day.'

Tom's father had moved into the flat after Tom's mother died. It had worked well. Tom was away a lot and his father's expertise had become crucial to the work he had been doing. They were a team and Tom enjoyed the closeness he felt when working on a project with his father.

'Absolutely, right and ready. Get cleaned up and I'll put on the coffee and the toast.'

Pop came out of his room and made his way to the kitchen. He was an older version of Tom, rugged, but still in good shape for his age, which was a little over thirty years older than his son. His years in the military had given him a sharpness, an edge, which he had not lost in the years after he left the service.

Tom had inherited some of his father's intensity. He was in his late thirties, broad shouldered, slim waisted, athletic with a boyish face.

Pop put some coffee on to brew and went back to the computer where he had taken over after Tom eventually went to sleep earlier that morning. The lounge of the flat looked out across rows of houses that faded into the grey dawn.

Tom, fresh from his shower, joined Pop in the lounge.

'How did it go last night?' asked Pop

'Not bad. I think I have a way of getting at that cash.'

Tom picked up a pack of printouts and handed it to Pop.

'Yes. I've taken a look at those. Interesting. What are we dealing with here, Son?'

'Dad, you remember Sally, from Chikangawa in Zim?'

'Yes, she was one of the big land owner's kids.'

'Yup, still is.'

'Is there trouble at Chikangawa?'

'Sally and the ranger there believe that some government fat cat wants to get to the Chikangawa ivory. It's probably the biggest herd in Africa, Dad, and the loss would mean the end of Chikangawa. Sally got some intelligence from Harare and she thinks this colonel is going to move on the Elephants within the next few days. It may even have begun already. Here, look at these. The herd was attacked by poachers yesterday.'

Tom handed Pop some aerial photographs he had received from Sally. They showed the herd and the area in detail. As Pop took the photographs from Tom he could see how serious his son was about this.

'That's a pretty big family. Where did you say this is?'

'Chikangawa, Pop. Southern Zimbabwe.' Tom ruffled through the paperwork to find a map of the area.

'So what is this telling me?'

'Take a look at the geo-survey data. Chikangawa lies only twenty kilometres north of the Zimbabwe/South African border. And look at the river depth of the Limpopo on the south-western side. See how shallow it is? Plus, the area is very sparsely populated. There are no roads except the paths used for border patrol.'

'You want to take the elephants over the border?'

'It's the only way to get them out by the end of the week. It's a long shot, but how else do we get the herd out en masse? We don't have the time or the manpower to arrange for trucking them out, and we can't rely on any help from the authorities.'

Tom handed Pop another sheet.

'This is Colonel Moroge, a war veteran from Zim's resistance struggle. It seems he's the man behind all of this.'

Pop skimmed the profile which had printed alongside the colonel's photograph.

'He was involved in the land grabs?'

'Dad, this guy is a bit of a challenge. He used to be at the top, but lately seems to have fallen from grace. One or two of my contacts have had dealings with him and he seems to be the kind of man who takes what he wants, whatever the expense. He is very connected and potentially very dangerous. We want to avoid running into him.'

The two men exchanged a glance. They had been in situations like this before, making decisions against the odds.

'So what do you think?'

'Son, it sounds like another of your half–baked, hair-brained schemes. Which means I'm in. What do you want me to do?'

'Well, you're the engineer in the family. I need to get a breakdown of everything we need to get this job done to Sally later today. She can gather the equipment down there and keep things below the radar. The less people who know what we are up to, the better.'

'And who will be paying for all of this?' This was always a tricky question. Pop smiled at Tom.

Tom walked over to the kitchen counter and picked up a magazine, which he passed to Pop. It was Global Petroleum's annual report.

'Okay, I'm listening.'

'You know, Pop, these oil companies have made a real mess in some of the beautiful places we've been to, and they don't seem to be sorry at all. Well I think I may have found a way to get them to support our little conservation business ... without their knowledge, of course.'

'What are you getting at?'

'Well. I've been working on something for a while now and if we move things along a little I think we can get our hands on a very large amount of cash within the next few days. We'll need some help though. I was hoping your mate Boris Bank Vault could help us.'

'Sure. You want me to get hold of him?'

'Yes, right now. We need to see him around lunchtime if possible. I want to be back here by three. Can you get him to bring a set of clean phones? I have a meeting this morning in the city and will meet you back here afterwards.'

Tom left his building in a hurry, oblivious to the cold morning air. Just down the road he jumped on a bus, which took him over Putney Bridge through Westminster and on to Strand Street, where he jumped off. After walking through the back streets past Covent Garden, he opened the door to a small bookshop filled with thousands of second-hand books, most of which were in a poor state.

Tom made his way to the back of the shop and went up a
narrow stairwell to a small flat above the shop. Knocking on the
door, he was welcomed in by a hunched man who looked older
in body than in face. His whispy grey hair was unbrushed and
his clothes were somewhat unkempt. The flat was over-furnished
with antiques and books covered every surface.

'Mr Jones.' Tom extended his hand and gave the man a smile.
'How are you doing? I am Tom Stone, we spoke on the phone.'

'Yes, Mr Stone. I remember, please take a seat.' Mr Jones
shuffled over to a coffee table piled high with books.

'Mr Jones, I have come about the information.'

'Yes, I have been keeping it for you.' The man shuffled up
to a bookshelf and rustled through envelopes that were piled
together. 'Here it is.' He handed Tom a large, stuffed brown
envelope.

Tom opened it, and skimmed its contents.

'Thank you, Mr Jones. You have been most helpful.' Tom made
to shake Mr Jones's hand as he stood up to leave.

'Please, Mr Stone, let me know how it goes. I have for many
years been waiting for this opportunity. I have a score of my own
to settle.'

'Well you've backed the right people. Thank you, Mr Jones.
I appreciate everything you've done.' Tom shook Mr Jones's
hand and made his way back down the narrow stairwell, his
heart beating fast as the pieces of his plan slowly started coming
together.

Tom made his way back out into the busy street and walked
the quarter mile to Fleet Street where he sat down at a coffee
shop and read the documents Mr Jones had given him.

'This is pretty good stuff. Let's hope it's accurate,' Tom thought
to himself.

After fully absorbing the contents of the documents, Tom paid
and made his way back out into the cold just as the rain started
to drizzle down on the mid-morning London traffic. Looking at
his watch, he crossed the road and entered an office building.
Shaking off the rain from his jacket he made his way into the
foyer reception.

A widemouthed receptionist greeted him.

'Good morning, Sir. How can I help you'?

'Good Morning. I am here to see Mr Benjamin. Please tell him it's Tom Stone.'

'I will call him, Sir. In the meantime, please fill out the register and take a seat.'

Tom made his way to the comfortable lounge and waited for his friend. Moments later a very business-like man emerged and made his way over to Tom.

'Michael, look at you!' Tom smacked him on the shoulder.

'Tom, good to see you. What are you doing here? Or shouldn't I ask?'

'Just came to see you. Can't an old mate pop in to say hi?'

'Well, even though you are an old mate, a visit usually means a trip and a trip usually means taking out more life insurance.'

Tom shrugged his shoulders, and, smiling, gave his friend a hug.

'Look at you, all suited up. Never seen you looking so smart.' Tom jokingly pulled at Mike's tie.

'We have a potential customer visiting today, an Arab sheikh wanting a charter contract to Saudi.'

'Nice, I hope it lands. I hate to rain on the parade, Mike, but I do need your help and I don't have much time.'

'I knew it. What's up?'

Tom and Mike made their way to a large couch in the corner where they could not be overheard.

'I need to get some elephants out of Zim, on foot, and I need you to give me a hand with some air support ... just your average illegal cross-border extraction of over two hundred elephant within the next three days.'

'You're joking. right?'

'Nope, this is the real thing. The stakes are high and it's going to be dangerous. I can't do this without you, Mike. I need you to trust me on the rest.'

'You're serious about this.'

'Don't make me beg, Mike. I need you, I need someone I can trust completely, and given you and I know all there is to know about each other, you are the only person other than Pop that I can trust with this.'

'And where may I ask are you getting the money for this hair-brained project you won't tell me anything about?'

'Never you mind, my friend. Having you on board makes all things possible. Meet me at my place this evening. I'll organise the rest. We should be back within a week.'

Tom stood up and affectionately punched his friend on the shoulder.

'And I assume the risks are the same as always?'

'Absolutely, but these are risks worth taking.'

With a broad smile, Tom walked across the lounge and back out into the busy Fleet Street traffic.

'Time to go home and pick up Pop.'

Tom hailed a black cab and drove across London back to his flat. Although the traffic was heavy, he made it back in good time and on opening the front door found Pop waiting for him, pouring over more printouts.

'How did it go, Son?'

'Went well. Mike is in, I got what I needed. How is the list going?'

'Not bad, I've finalised an inventory and made contact with some of my mates in South Africa. The wheels are turning.'

'Excellent. Thankyou, Pop.'

'Good news about Mike. And your other meeting?'

'Have a look at this, Pop.'

Tom handed him the envelope he received from Mr Jones. While Pop read, Tom made himself a sandwich and went to his computer to check his email.

'Son, this is some good stuff. I can't believe some of the things these oil companies are willing get themselves into.'

'These guys will do anything for money and to show a profit for their shareholders. What they are doing in Nigeria is criminal.'

'Who is Mr Jones'?

'He was head of security at Amexo. He used to look after their drilling in Nigeria and the reserves off the coast. Things went wrong though, and now he's a converted conservationist. He's an ally, a friend.'

'What do you mean?'

'Well, here's the story. Mr Jones arrived in Nigeria around the time when the oil companies were striking agreements with warlords, chiefs and politicians. It was a free for all, and everybody was getting rich ... everyone except the local population, that is. The agreements were all sensitive, and every now and again Amexo had to renegotiate with cash handouts. This is standard procedure and is how things still get done today. Mr Jones was in charge of security for two key wells and for important personnel. He was also tasked with looking after payments to the warlords, none of whom had bank accounts and preferred cash ... in American dollars.'

'So he was in charge of bribery to drum up support for Amexo drilling the pipeline?'

'That's absolutely right. The pipeline delivered oil to the coast where it was shipped off and eventually, after some refinement, turned into a very tidy profit for Amexo shareholders. The pipeline was built through some of the most sensitive ecological areas on the continent and there was massive destruction of the environment. Money paid to chieftains and warlords was used to buy weapons, which in turn were used to oppress the local people; the result of which was the killing of over a hundred thousand civilians.'

Pop shook his head. 'And Amexo turned a blind eye.'

'Of course, Pop. They denied any involvement in providing local warlords with money to protect the pipeline and also denied any allegations of their involvement in the environmental destruction, instead blaming the Nigerian economy.'

'Sad story, Son. What does this mean for us?'

'Well, fortunately for us, Mr Jones has a score to settle. After years of service he was fired and badly roughed up after an incident in which he let a group of civilians go after they had stolen food from one of the pipeline depot food stores. The civilians involved had been accused of sabotage by local warlords, but Mr Jones knew that the sabotage had been part of a warlord struggle.'

'Mr Jones decided to go to the press, but he was badly beaten and his family was at risk, so he decided to retract his story. He's a bitter old man.'

'And how did you get to him'?

'A journalist friend of mine followed his story. I managed to get a contact number and after dropping a few names eventually got to talk to Mr Jones.'

'I'm dying to hear how this leads us to the cash.'

'Well, Pop, Mr Jones believes Amexo is still moving large amounts of cash for bribing the warlords. Lucky for us, they store the money here in London and move it out in shipments every six months … around five million dollars in unmarked, weathered bills.'

'No Swiss bank account?'

'Apparently not. Cash is still king. And completely untraceable. Amexo looks clean, the warlords ensure that the pipeline remains operational and the shareholders are happy.'

'Sounds like a solid Robin Hood hit to me'.

'Bad news is that the transfer team is highly trained and armed, I would rather bag this one at storage, which brings me to your friend, Boris.'

'Mr Jones has given us the storage address, the specs for the safe, a map of the facility and the guarding schedule.'

'Sounds pretty comprehensive. A little too good to be true.'

'Yes, well there is one catch.'

'And what would that be?'

'We need to do it tonight.'

Chapter 6
BORIS THE RUSSIAN

**14h50, Thursday 13 September –
The Barrackade, A Popular Night Club**

POP AND Tom entered the West End nightclub. Shaking off their wet raincoats, they made their way through the almost deserted club. Except for some cabaret dancers stretching on the stage before rehearsals, the place was dark and stank of stale smoke and beer. Pop led the way and took Tom through the back doors, through a makeshift kitchen and out a back entrance to a cobblestone yard. On the other side of the yard was what looked like an old jail. It was a stone building with high barred windows and a very solid-looking broad-beam door, and it seemed to stand alone, not attached to the surrounding buildings at all. Its roof was flat and it was only a single storey high. It also seemed to have battlements on the roof that had been redesigned into a castle-like feature.

'Very James Bond, Pop.'

'I suppose it's ironic,' chuckled Pop, 'that Boris lives in a renovated jailhouse from the eighteen hundreds.'

'Definitely one of your more enigmatic friends. What's with the club?'

'Boris's nest egg. He makes a pretty penny out of it too.'

Arriving at the door, Pop used a large brass knocker to alert Boris to their presence.

The door was quickly opened by one of the smallest men Tom had ever seen. For a safe-cracking Russian military man, he hardly looked the part. Standing at around five-and–a-half feet, Boris had thick red hair that also covered his jaw line. He looked like a leprechaun.

'Friends, friends, come in, this is shocking weather.' Boris greeted them warmly in his deep rolling Russian accent.

'It is good to see you, old friend!' Pop held Boris by each shoulder and they embraced before shaking hands.

'Tom.' Boris grabbed Tom's hand, and even though the small Russian was just over half of Tom's height, his grip was extremely strong. 'It is good to finally meet you. Come in, both of you, pull off those raincoats.'

Boris took their coats and they moved into what seemed like a medieval castle of sorts, each room walled in thick stone with solid wood furnishings that were all a bit rustic. The floors were also made of thick cut stone, but were warmed by layers of woollen rugs. In the corner of the entrance area was a large open fireplace with a blazing fire. Through a short hall, which could have been the entrance to where the jailers used to live, was a very comfortable lounge. Large leather chairs, rugs and some beautiful tapestries, which looked rather valuable, filled the room. In the corner was a circular stairwell going down to the dungeon. The stairs were huge, at least two meters long and a meter wide at the end. A glow of light illuminated what used to be the cells. The jail house had lost its once musty scent of sweat and mould, which had been replaced by the strong yet pleasant aroma of brewing coffee.

'Was this really a jail house?' asked Tom while they walked through to the lounge.

'Young Tom, this was one of the first Jails built in London, dates back to Roman times and has been rebuilt a few times. It was going to be demolished, but I managed to pull a few strings.'

'Please come and sit down.' Boris escorted them to the lounge.

'How about some coffee?'

Both visitors agree to a hot cup. Boris walked over to a counter that ran the length of the lounge, which was filled with stainless steel kitchen appliances, fridges, microwaves, stove with an extractor fan, a large coffee machine and an enormous sink.

The coffee smelled delicious and when Boris had finished filling the cups, he brought round a tray and offered both Tom and Pop some delectable Russian teacakes, filled with a rich flavour which must have been some sort of liqueur.

'So, gentlemen, what is so urgent that we needed to meet at such short notice?'

'Tom, you go ahead.' Pop gestured with an open hand to Boris.

'We have a job for you Boris, but this is something that needs to happen immediately.' Tom and Boris exchanged a knowing glance.

'I see. And by immediately you mean?'

'Tonight' grimaced Tom.

Boris started to laugh, a deep gruff laugh that came bubbling out of him. This carried on for some time, leaving Tom and Pop smiling at each other.

'My friends, there is no way that I can pull a job tonight ... or for the next two weeks. Preparation aside, I am singing at the Albert Hall tonight.'

Boris looked very pleased with himself. He had been a long-standing member of a renowned male choir, an occupation that saw him travelling through Europe and Asia extensively.

'Is there any way we could convince you?'

'Not a very big chance of that I am afraid, but why do you not tell me of the plan and I will see what I can help with.'

'We need a safe cracked tonight. Here are the specs of the mini-vault' Tom handed Boris some of the material that Mr Jones had given him. Boris studied it intensely, his interest piqued.

'This is an older unit, should be fairly easy to crack, but why my good friends would you want to crack this safe?'

Pop looked at Tom and smiled. 'Go ahead.'

Tom smiled and began his explanation while Boris listened intently. After hearing about the Colonel, Boris was suddenly a whole lot more interested. Boris knew how things were in Zimbabwe and was a sworn enemy of petroleum companies. Tom could see he was warming to the idea. When he finished his story, wrapping up with the background on Mr Jones, Boris took off his glasses, pulled out his glasses case and, using a small cloth from inside, slowly cleaned the lenses, deep in thought.

'Gentlemen, this safe can be opened fairly easily, but I would have to do it myself. If I were to help you out, I would need safe entry and exit, and a job like this needs careful planning. Our problem is not so much the safe, but access. These guys are going to be well trained and will come down hard if we're discovered. Tom, you know I support your effort and would follow your father into battle, but this is the big time. You're proposing that we mess with some serious guys here.'

'Boris, I understand that it is a dangerous undertaking, but if we can't access the money tonight, it's the end of that herd. I can't let that happen. What if we did the job with help from you on the outside?'

'Determined, like your father, I see.' Boris scratched his brow. 'It could work, but we have no guarantees. For me this is not a difficult safe, but I have had two decades of experience. And if things go wrong, the good times will go very bad.'

'If you did the work on the safe and we paved the way for easy entry and exit, how long would it take to open?' asked Pop.

'A few minutes. I have the blueprint for this one downstairs. Let's go down and have a look.' Boris stood up and made his way to the corner stairwell.

Tom and Pop followed down the stairs into a large dungeon. Except for a number of thick stone support pillars the entire concrete floor was open. On the far wall there were neatly laid out tools of every kind on three levels of shelving which ran the extent of the wall. On the right side were many filing cabinets and in the far corner a number of computer stations and what looked like a server cabinet with flashing lights. Boris joined the military during the Cold War and later worked for the KGB, a bright young technician whose job it was to assist agents in the field with technical information on buildings, safes, tunnels and information systems. Anything that had some design behind it. Having developed an interest in code cracking and safe breaking, Boris did all of his own work and soon became involved in counter intelligence as an agent, but this did not last long as Boris was keen on living in a free world. He hoped for a better life in the west and a chance to pursue his passion of singing. On a trip to England in the 1990s he decided to seize his chance, walking into a British Secret Service branch and handing himself over. After a lengthy relocation and debriefing which lasted six months, Boris was allowed to settle in the United Kingdom.

Boris had a love of the wild from his boyhood spent in a village on the outskirts of a forest and the roughness of the Scottish Highlands suited him well. This was also where he first started really using the internet, making friends with a few people who were prepared to go to some extreme lengths to protect what they loved.

Boris had heard of an organisation that had started to fund the purchase of large tracts of land in Scotland and England, where all buildings, power lines and roads were to be removed and behind well managed fences, animals like badgers, foxes, rabbits, voles, toads, tortoises and many others could flourish again. In all cases millions of British Pounds were being used to buy the land and hire the skills necessary to create a balanced ecosystem. The organisation seemed to exist in the background and was very careful about its members. Boris attempted to join, as this was the type of organisation that he felt he could add value to. It took the better part of two years before he was able to make contact with Pop Stone. Membership was carefully assessed by the organisation that was for all purposes nameless, but for those in the know who called it CI, short for Conserva Internationale. As members, all your special skills were brought to bear on initiatives across the globe. Boris was one member who had skills that could be used for cash generation. It was not long before Boris had gained the trust of both Tom and Pop and had become a member of the inner circle. Here decisions were taken on what projects needed money and in many cases money was channelled away from organisations and countries that were committing crimes against the environment. This was the new philosophy that Boris had adopted, an environmental conscience that he saw as his salvation, especially after all the years he had supported a regime that caused the death and destruction of much of the wild Russia he had loved as a boy.

It was because of this relationship that trust between Pop, Tom and Boris was without question and more so now than ever before as the actions and activities of Conserva Internationale were becoming more controversial as more and more money was being redistributed. A list of countries and companies had been created, a hit list of repeat offenders who had, for reasons of money or power, sacrificed the natural world and in many cases local peoples too, all for commercial gain. Those on the list met key criteria and if you were on the list then it was open season. Those on the list included corrupt countries that consumed and destroyed the environment for their own personal gain, where the rule of law was merely for their own upliftment and enrichment. The list also included companies that caused environmental damage for shareholder value, including those that poached wild animals for profit, like whalers, seal-skin traders and ivory and rhino horn hunters.

They were at war for the environment, for all those creatures that seemingly had no rights, and Boris had become one of the most important inner circle members. With his connections, many of them retained from his war days, Boris had been directly responsible for raising millions of dollars for conservation projects across the globe. This old jailhouse had become the base for all Boris's work to support Tom and the rest of the growing team. Even though Tom and Boris had known each other for years, they had never met in person, sticking to the organisation's code of keep channels of communication and networks as oblique as possible. They had invested heavily in protecting themselves and the organisation. These were exceptional circumstances.

Boris walked over to a large computer screen and sat down in a comfortable leather chair. He moved the mouse and the machine came to life. He typed in a few details in a search box and out popped streams of data – schematics and pictures of the safe in question. It was a large safe, with two compartments that were each the size of a gurney. This enabled larger objects to be wheeled in as required.

'Only five of this type of safe were made; all by hand, in Italy.' Boris scanned the specs and background data on the safe, clearly in his element.

'Here!' Boris excitedly pointed to a schematic he had pulled up. 'This is why it was not a big seller The wheel lock has a weakness, with only three variants to the roller, making it possible to break open the safe with a stethoscope and a drill pack. If there have been no enhancements, it should be a walk in the park ... though I don't like to tempt fate. But anyway it is not for you to do. You have to be able to feel the safe to do these things, and we do not have the time for me to show you such things. I would have to listen to the mechanism as the wheel was being turned.'.

'It must be a pretty big vault if they can park a truck inside it?' Pop asked

'It is big. The vault is usually a large area that is concreted in and this unit is placed in as a door. The door unit includes a safe ventilation system, but even with this feature it did not sell. Price and pickability always a problem.' Boris smiled. 'Italians make very good engineers, but I think the size of this one made it a bit of a, how do you say, a white elephant.' Boris coughed out a laugh.

'So what do we do about you?' Tom asked Boris

'What sort of money are we looking at?' Boris looked at Pop who had always been the money man in the family.

'Looks like around three thousand pounds per elephant for the truck transfers from the border to the new reserve.' Pop took out a printout from his pocket, and pulled out his glasses.

'The costs for transfer of the whole herd will be around a three quarters of a million pounds and with all the ground support, veterinary skills and bribe money we probably in for a cool million.' Pop looked up at Boris over his glasses.

'Well I guess me lending you the money is out of the question then. Things have definitely changed. We used to be able to pull these things off with a little sweat and a hitched ride on someone else's plane.' Boris got up from the computer and moved across to a window to see the moon rising in the freezing London sky.

'OK, how much is in the safe?' he asked.

'Around two million pounds. There may be more, but based on what Mr Jones has told us the shipments are usually for three or four warlords at a time, with five hundred thousand pounds for each'. Tom smiled at Boris. 'Fits nicely, doesn't it?'

Boris shook his head and muttered under his breath, but Tom knew they had him.

'Alright,' he said eventually, 'if we work on this for the next two hours, it may be possible. Talk me through your plan.' Boris took out a handkerchief and wiped his brow

Tom pulled out some more documents from his folder, one of which was a detailed map of the depot, and opened them onto a large oak table in the middle of the room, The three men leaned over them.

'Boris, this is the plan. Late night security consists of four well-armed guards ... two in a security office where they man the closed-circuit cameras, the other two do gate duty and they seem to swap over half way through the night. There is only one way into the vault complex, and it seems the depot is also used to store equipment. We have reason to believe that they're planning to move the money tomorrow, which means the truck is already inside the depot. They would, I assume from Mr Jones, be using these filter trays as transport for the money. Once packed, they would be almost undetectable if searched as each filter tray for the pipeline will be welded shut, the money being hidden in insulated pockets.'

'You say it is in US dollars?' asked Boris.

'Yes, that seems to be the desirable currency.'

Boris looked down at the map again as Tom continued. 'We have to immobilise the gate guards and the two in the security room at the same time so we'll use darts. The two at the gate are easy enough to get a clear shot at, and there is an air inlet to the security room's air conditioner at the back of the building so we can gain access there. Knock them out for an hour or two. Entry then is with a big pair of gate cutters and then it's over to you.'

'What about the cameras?' asked Boris.

'We get to play a little dress-up and wear masks. Let the cameras roll. They can at least have a story to tell their families.'

Boris patted Tom on the shoulder. He liked this boy who was so much like his father when Boris first met him. 'Lets go over that map again.' Boris pulled out some transparency paper and made some notes and drawings, capturing everything in some strange mathematical language.

The three men worked into the evening, going over the plan repeatedly until they all knew exactly what to do and when to do it. Just after six in the evening, Boris turned to Tom and smiled. 'We should be able to do this, my boy.'

Tom smiled back at Boris. 'I am glad to hear it.'

Making final arrangements, Tom and Pop agreed to meet Boris at the vault facility in four hours. Tom and Pop would need to get the dart guns and other kit from a storage garage in Greenwich Village and then make their way back to central London.

Chapter 7
Getting Some Cash

23h40, Thursday 13 September –
Outside a High-Tech Islington Compound

TOM AND Pop arrived on foot, each carrying a large black shoulder bag. Both Tom and Pop were wearing dark blue overalls. Stopping down the road from the compound, Tom gave the gate house a quick look.

'Looks like Mr Jones was on the money, his plan seems to fit what we are looking at, what do you think Pop?'

'From the outside yes, but what does it look like on the inside' Pop answered.

'We will only find that out when we get inside, here's hoping we are on track' Tom lifted the bag back onto his shoulder and started walking on past the compound gates. Pop remained where he was.

Tom looked through the diamond mesh gates into the compound as he breezed past. The layout was as expected, but there were a few additional trucks parked inside. Tom lifted his hand to his throat, holding a microphone pad onto his skin

'Pop can you hear me?'

'Yup, read you, what's it look like?'

'Fine, but we have a few unexpected guests, a few other trucks. Not sure whether there are attached drivers or guards, but even so we should be able to get in and out easily enough'

'Sure, after you pass, I will set up across the road' Pop threw the black bag over his shoulder and started walking up the road.

'Good stuff, I am going around back to meet Boris, switch your radio off for fifteen, will call you as soon as we are in'

'Okie dokie' Pop replied 'Go slow my boy' Pop switched his radio off and pulled into the covered entrance of a closed fish and chip shop, directly across from the gate of the compound. Pulling out a small black rollerbag, he removed a small silver pick, opened the door and went inside.

Tom waited for only a few minutes at the corner until Boris arrived. He too was wearing a dark blue overall, under it his black tuxedo

'How was the show?' Tom asked

'Delectable, took me to how should I say, a paradise' Boris answered in his thick Russian accent

'You ready for this evenings alternative entertainment'

'For sure, I am excited, been some time'

'Well, the layout looks good, but we may have some additional personnel, two additional trucks outside, may be asleep in the compound and we are not too sure if they are just drivers or also armed guards'

'We will just have to be extra careful'

Tom handed Boris his headset and as he was sliding it onto his belt and guiding the wires up to his ear and throat, Tom unpacked the two dart guns and loaded each with the tranquilisers.

'How long for them to fall asleep?'

'Thirty seconds, but if they are already sleeping, they will most probably just rub it like it was a bite. The darts fall off immediately, unless they get stuck in their clothes. We must just shoot well today

Tom passed Boris one of the guns

'These are nice, well balanced and nicely weighted, how quiet?' Boris looked at Tom

'Very, sounds like a beer opening' Tom smiled

'Then I am going to get thirsty listening'

'High pressure gas in the back, high power, range of fifty meters before it becomes inaffective, not bad'

'How many cartridges?'

'Here are three more magazines, each one has six darts. You can fire one at a time or rapid fire them one after the other

'I have also brought some additional firepower' Boris pulled out a small automatic pistol from behind his back.

'Boris, use it only if things get rough. I want this to be a silent theft. The authorities will most probably never know and these guys will wake in an hour or two not knowing what happened. If we leave the safe locked and everything undisturbed, they may even wonder if they imagined being drugged'

'Unlikely my boy' Boris smiled

'So where do we get in?'

'Just up there, there is a fence line, electrified on top but we can get in underneath, wire cutters' Tom passed Boris a pair

'Thanks, let's get going'

'One last thing'

'What's that'

'A mask for those cameras, there are a few we know of, all onto recording equipment, rather leave no trace

'Good idea, hate to have to explain this'

'Me too' answered Tom with a smile

'Just have to let pop know and we can test our radios, just about time for Pop to switch back on'

'Pop are you there?'

'Reading you Tom, hi Boris'

'Yup radio working well'

'Pop we are ready to go, all well with you'

'Yes, been watching and there has been no movement, can see the guard house but not a peep, maybe those boys are sleeping or watching a movie, but all is clear'

'Thanks Pop, we are on our way, keep us informed of anything on the outside'

'Will do, good luck'

'Thanks'

'We don't need luck, we have a good cause that will steer us' Boris commented

Tom walked up to the fence line and started cutting through. Boris joined him and within a few minutes they had opened up a hole wide enough for them to get through. Tom stuck his head through and looked up and down the side of the compound.

'There are no cameras I can see, looks like Jonesy is still on the money'

'Good, lets move'

Boris and Tom climbed through into the compound and kneeling on the ground, they both looked and listened carefully before moving down the meter wide approach corridor to the compound parking. Half way along they passed large electricity transformer boxes.

'The compound power boxes also the backup power in case of a blackout' Tom whispered to Boris, pointing at two large green cupboards that were buzzing

'Jones was on the money, lets hope they have not updated the electronics of the vault'

Boris put down his bag and pulling open a Velcro pouch, pulled out a small explosive charge

'A bit stupid to put the backup power box right next to the mains power, just asking for trouble' Boris smiled at Tom

'We can set this off when we are inside; it has a range of around a hundred meters' Boris used a square key to open the transformer boxes and he attached the charge to the inside of the door with a magnetic strip. Carefully opening a small plastic cover, Boris armed it and then closed up like no one had been there.

'Looks good' Tom signalled thumbs up

'Once she blows, hopefully the vault will be ours and the security system will be blind' Boris packed away his tools and closed his bag

After loading the charge, Tom led the way with Boris behind to the opening at the end of the corridor. From the shadows, Tom looked across the compound. A large high watt flood light shone over the parking area where the two armoured cars were parked. From the window of the guard house at the end of the parking, guards had an open and clear view of everything in the compound. The only entry areas were the two corridors on opposite sides of the compound, which led to storage cupboards on one side and the electricity boxes on the other.

'Can you see anyone in there' Boris asked

'No, there is a bit of a reflection from the light outside, I do not want to risk it.' Tom looked across to where the two trucks were parked

'If we can get in behind those, we will be clear all the way up to the door'

'So what's your plan if they see us?'

'Run like hell, those guys have real guns, I don't want to end my days here'

'So how will we be sure they can not see us?'

'Boris, I promised you I would get you in, leave the rest to me'

Tom pulled up his radio and changed the channel to a frequency Jones had given him. Then sitting on his haunches, he listened.

'There we go, get ready Boris, we will have to move in a few seconds' Tom stood up and grabbed Boris by the shoulder

'How do you know it is clear?'

'Sixth sense and the info Jonesy gave us, the guards change at midnight and the guards booth is empty for a few minutes as they swop over most probably chatting at the coffee machine.'

Tom gave the signal and both men ran across the open compound until they had reached the cover of the two trucks, which were parked in front of the large roller doors through to the main vault, where the money truck was parked. Tom knelt down behind one of the trucks and signalled Boris to keep his eyes open for movement in the booth. A few minutes later they saw the shape of two men enter and sit down. The reflection from the security light was on the other side now and they had a clear view of what was going on in the booth.

'Boris, we have to get to the door on the left of the booth. There is a security window just inside that door. It is open and we should be able to get clear shots at those two in the booth'

'Got you' Boris signalled with a thumbs up

Tom crawled down the length of the truck that was opposite the guard's booth and stopped when he could see them round the front bumper. Tom waited for them to turn their backs and he signalled Boris. Both of them ran to the door and crouched in the shadows. On Toms signal, Boris picked the lock on the door and opened it slowly. Inside was a wide corridor, at the end of which they could see a large vault door in shiny steel. To their right was the guard's booth, which had large windows on the inside as well as outside. It was supposed to be used to provide a security solution that could see the entire compound and keep an eye on the vault, but these guards were overconfident. Doors were left open and just above Tom and Boris was an open security grate.

Tom pointed up as he lay up against the wall with his shoulders and Boris responded with a nod. Tom rolled over and getting into a crouching position, cocked his dart gun. Signalling three two one, they both slid up from behind the counter and through the open grate, aimed and fired two shots each at the two guards in the booth.

'Shit! What was that?' One guard shouted, turning around

'Flipping hell, that hurt' the other guard rubbed his back

'What was that?' the two guards spun around on their chairs looking for what had stung them

'Someone playing silly buggers I think' The one guard stood up and was about to move across to the open grate, but suddenly sat down again.

'Whew, I am a bit dizzy, too much coffee' he rubbed his head.

Amazingly, neither guard looked down to the ground. There lay four small compression darts.

The guards looked around but Tom and Boris had slipped down silently to the ground below the counter. Tom was counting in his head to thirty seconds. Tom waited and on hearing two soft thuds, slid up to take a look. Both guards were lying on the floor, out cold.

'Should give us a half hour or so, now for the others, down to the dormitory and cafeteria'

'After you my boy' signalled Boris

The corridor led directly to the vault and on their right through intermediate pillars was a concrete driveway so that a full sized truck could be stowed away in the vault.

Tom made his way slowly down the corridor, with Boris close behind. Both were in combat stance pointing their guns at any potential threats. The dormitory room where the guards slept was just ahead on the left, followed by a bathroom and then a small kitchen area and a table. Tom could hear two men talking at the end of the corridor. Hopefully if the drivers were on site they would be sleeping. Tom signalled to Boris that he was going into the dormitory room. Opening it slowly Tom could see it was dark inside. Slipping in quietly he closed the door behind him and stood very still at the entrance, waiting for his eyes to adjust to the light. Boris stood at the door. The room had six bunk styled beds, two in each corner and a make shift cupboard in the fourth corner. The room smelt of stale cigarettes. Two of the double bunks were empty, but on the top of the remaining bunk was an overweight man asleep. Tom could hear him breathing deeply. Making his way across the room, Tom could smell the man's breathe. He had been drinking

'This crew is really slack' Tom thought to himself.

Taking aim, he fired two darts into the man's shoulder. The darts fell away to the ground and with a short grunt and groan the man turned from his side onto his back and started snoring. Tom waited, wondering if such a large man would need more than two darts. There was no need, within thirty seconds his breathing lightened to only a soft whisper.

Tom opened the door

'Three down and a few more to go'

'How many did Jones say there were?'

'Five at most, I think that is about right'

Tom and Boris checked the bathroom but it was dark and empty. After walking slowly down the length of the corridor, Tom stopped short of where the kitchen opened up. Tom peeped around the corner. With a quick signal to Boris that there were two men seated, they both jumped out and fired two more shots each.

'Hey, what are you doing!' shouted one of the men. He stood from his seat and drew a revolver and aimed it at Tom. He had two darts embedded in his chest. The other man had two darts from Boris's gun stuck in his back.

'Shit they have got bullet-proofs on, fire again' Tom shouted as he moved quickly across the front of the kitchen. Firing again, Tom managed to catch the standing man with a single dart in the neck. The guard, a tall strong looking man fired three shots, but Tom was moving too quickly and managed to take cover behind a pillar.

Boris backed off behind the wall and fired three more shots from a full magazine before hitting the other guard on the leg. He had also stood up but did not have a gun. Both guards had now jumped behind the kitchen counter. Toms hit would work quickly, but the other man may take a few minutes.

'Who the fuck are you guys, what do you want?' shouted one of the guards

The other guard was shouting for help, but nobody came. His shouts became more garbled as the drugs took effect. The bigger man had already dropped into a coma, the drugs making their way directly into his artery through his neck.

Boris stood on lookout and had taken his automatic pistol out just in case. A minute passed and everything grew quiet again

'Clear?' Boris shouted

'Should be, good shooting, nearly got into trouble there, why these guys are wearing their vests off duty, I will never know?' Tom answered as he walked across to check on the two drugged men

'Yup they are out cold, hopefully that is the lot of them'

'I haven't seen anyone else' Boris replied and he holstered his automatic

'Strange crew, very slack but in their kevlar' Tom looked quizzically at Boris

'Yes, not the brightest, cant buy good help these days, no wonder they never gave these clowns access to the vault, would have been a disaster'

'On that note' Tom turned and in front of them was a three meter diameter door. It was covered in polished stainless steel and had a small wheel in the bottom centre. There was a key hole and a combination wheel lock

'How does it look Boris?'

'It is original; this is going to be easy'

Boris made his way to the door and checked all the components. Pulling from his bag a drill and a stethoscope, he looked carefully below the centre of the wheel

'Here is the weak point, if I go through here, I will be able to see the lock in action and play with the mechanism, but I need some power failure'

'You say when and I will let her blow'

'Give me two minutes to set up, can you give me a hand with these lights' Boris passed Tom two high powered battery powered camp lights. Tom set them up at an angle behind Boris, giving him uninterrupted light.

'How are we doing for time?' Boris asked while he attached his suction cup drill base to the door

'We are looking good, two minutes ahead of the game'

'Better tell your father'

'Will do'

Tom switched channels again

'Pop, you there'

'Sure son, are you in'

'Yes, easy as pie, are you ready to get us out of here'

'Will make my way to the back, it has been as quiet as can be up here'

'Where is the car?'

'I parked it earlier this afternoon one block down from the rear entrance. Will take me a minute to get down there, I will meet you at the fence.'

'Great, will signal you when we are ready to leave the compound, will be a few minutes then until we are back at the fence'

'Sure thing' Pop signed off and made his way back out into the cold. There had been only a few passers by, but the night had been very quiet.

'Tom' Boris called 'I am almost ready for you'

'Give me the word'

'OK go for it'

Tom pressed a button on a small transmitter. The lights went off immediately.

'OK Boris, now we are on the clock. The security company will be notified of the power failure. They will be here in fifteen minutes based on driving distance.'

'More than enough time' Boris answered

Boris stuck the stethoscope to his ear and listened as he turned the combination wheel. After a few turns, he switched on the drill and made a small hole just beneath the centre of the mechanism wheel. The special drill pulsated and cut through the metal like it was butter. Removing the drill, Boris pulled out a small ocular scope that he slid into the hole. It had a light at the end. Looking at a small screen, Boris started to turn the combination wheel clockwise and then anticlockwise. This he did three times until there was a click.

'Now for the safety lock'

Boris pulled out an old looking key from his jacket pocket, and slid it into to the keyhole

'This is the moment of truth' Boris whispered as he turned the key

The lock gave another click and Boris spun the wheel and with a thud the door opened. The door weighed well over a ton, but was on a specially designed hinge that would allow even a small child to open it.

'That's why you are the best Boris'

Boris bowed and standing up again smiled

'All for a good cause my boy, all for a good cause'

Inside as expected there was an armoured truck

Boris quickly made his way to the back of the truck, where he inspected the time lock mechanism, and pulling from his bag

His final trick, he attached a large magnetic box. Pressing a few buttons on a console, he took it off again and pulled at the handle

'Hey presto' Boris smiled. The door swung open

'How did you do that?' asked Tom

'These things are easy, fitted with a magnetic time lock. I used a magnetic inhibitor to change the clock and set it to the date of delivery. It would automatically open the inner lock at that time, allowing someone with a magnetic strip card to open the outer lock and we're in'

'You're a genius Boris'

'I know but save the praise until later, we need to get out of here'

Tom climbed into the truck and opening a trolley box, pulled out from the top a black bag. Cutting the seal he unzipped it and inside saw what they had come for. American Dollars!

'Is it right?' asked Boris

'Looks like it, not sure how much, but should be enough given the notes are in fifties and hundreds' Tom pulled out a large wad of notes and flicked through.

'Unmarked, non sequential?' asked Boris

'Better than that, old used notes, the real thing, oil companies have some of the best cash laundries I can assure you of that'

'Let's get out of here'

Tom sealed up the trolley and wheeled it out from inside the truck. Boris dropped his bag on top of the trolley and pulled out his automatic again and the two men made their way towards the front of the compound. All the guards remained sleeping.

'This has to be the easiest gig in town'

'That it is; but they never expected that anyone would know of the moneys existence, especially seeing as these guys have never been hit or so they say'

The compound was dark and quiet as they wheeled the trolley out to where they had come in. Boris had closed up the safe leaving it as they had found it. Even when the guards awoke, they would not be able to confirm the theft until morning as the timelock on the truck had been reset by Boris.

Pop was waiting at the fence with the car behind him. Boris and Tom unloaded the money bags, as the trolley would not fit through the fence.

'That went well' Tom looked at Boris and Pop 'Thanks Boris, we could not have done that without you, you must be the only man alive that could have done that'

'It was my pleasure, but remember, I am counting on that money going to good use'

'You have my word' Tom turned to face Boris.

'I want to get back home and to bed, this has been far too exciting for me'

'Boris, you once again have made everything possible' Tom held out his open hand.

'My boy, for you and your projects, it is only my pleasure', Boris winked and then grabbed Toms hand with a firm grip and gave it two quick shakes.

'Good job boys' Pop patted both Tom and Boris on the shoulder

'Nobody got hurt and Amexo even gets to spend some money on its corporate environmental program.'

Five minutes later with a boot full of stolen oil bribery money, Tom, Boris and Pop pulled out from the side of the compound, and drove through the quiet streets of London.

Chapter 8
ON TO ZIMBABWE

03h30 – Friday 14 September – A Garage in South London

TOM STONE was sitting on the edge of a soft couch, sipping a warm mug of tea and chewing on a crunchy. The room was comfortably furnished for a garage, with two singe beds, a couch, TV, bathroom, kitchen counter with a microwave, fridge and kettle, and a large safe. Pop was sleeping nearby and packing large wooden boxes in the corner was a short red-haired man in his thirties.

'Want a crunchy, Rust?' Tom asked

'You bet. It's been a long night waiting for you and all.'

'Sorry, Rust. We had an appointment with those Amexo guys who so kindly offered to assist us with our plan. Nice to have friends like that to help you out at short notice, don't you think?'

'Uh-huh.'

Tom handed Rusty some of Pop's finest.

Rusty was the nickname all his friends had given him. Russell Smith was his name and special effects were his best game. He had worked for some of the top film production companies over the last few years and had made his mark as one of the best explosive FX men in the business. Exploding buildings, weapons fire in war movies, big-scene shots of battlefields ... this was Rusty's territory. He and Tom had been at school together had built up a trust that was unbreakable. They shared a love for adventure and Rusty had supported Tom in his projects whenever he was called upon, which, lately, was often.

'How much have we stowed so far?' Tom asked

'About one-and-a-half million. Could do a lot with that, how much has Pop budgeted?'

'Around two million for the whole thing, but looking at that haul it seems we may be a bit short.'

'I don't know. I think we might make it.'

'But can you fit it all in?'

'Sure, we have twenty small boxes with SFX light explosives. Each has a middle section that looks like solid wood but will hide around a hundred thousand bucks. I will also be carrying some cash and I have left two envelopes for you and Pop ... ten thousand each, should it be needed.'

'Great.' Tom sat up, taking the envelopes from the table and tucking them into his and Pop's bags.

'Ok, so only half-a-million to go. I doubt that these pyro-boxes will be checked too closely. They're booked onto a special flight carrying the rig for a film being shot in South Africa which leaves in about four hours. Customs in South Africa should pass the whole bang shoot without a problem, especially with Pop's contact there overseeing things. They're pretty lenient anyway when the paperwork is done right and they hate touching explosives, especially when they're earmarked for a shoot. Don't want to jeopardise any costly production schedules or anything.' Rusty smiled. 'Once the stuff gets to the other side, it should clear customs in a few hours.' I'll be accompanying it and if everything goes according to plan we should have the shipment cleared by the time you and Pop land.

'Excellent. I've chartered a plane to get us up to the border. Mike will meet us there with some air support. He arrived in Johannesburg this morning and has been setting things up, working his magic.' Tom and Rusty exchanged a knowing smile. The stakes were high, but it made all the difference going into the situation with friends you could trust. Tom would put his life in Mike or Rusty's hands any day.

'Okay, so it looks like we're about ready. We'd better get moving. I'll help you pack the van. This stuff going with you as well?' Tom pointed to a heavy-duty camera case and a few well-worn ruck sacks in the corner.

'Yip, my camera … and a few additional surprises, should we need a little reinforcement.'

There was movement on the bunk. Pop was awake.

'Hey, Pop. Sleep well?'

'Not enough, but will hopefully catch up on the plane. What time is it?'

'Almost four.'

'Hi Pop' Rusty waved.

'Hey Russell, you still packing? Been a long night for you.'

'Not as exciting as yours, Pop. We're almost done here.'

Rusty tucked a block of dollars into the last of the explosives boxes and sealed it thoroughly.

'So let's get out of here. The guys at the cargo carriers depot will be expecting me.'

Pop climbed from his bed, pulled on a jacket and lined up. The three passed boxes in a line and stacked them behind the van. Rusty then climbed into the van and took each box that Tom passed to him, stacked them carefully inside the van. The side of the van had all the necessary official signage reading 'Dangerous Cargo' and 'Explosives in Transit' and Rusty had prepared all the paperwork should he be pulled over by the authorities.

Once the van was packed and Rusty had stowed all his other equipment in the van, he jumped in and started her up. Tom smiled and waved goodbye without a word.

'Good luck, see you on the other side.' Pop banged on the side of the van as Rusty drove out of the garage into the cold, misty London morning.

'We had better get moving too. Our flight is at eight and we have a lot to do. First, I need to check in with Sally to confirm we are on schedule.'

Tom walked to the corner and picked up a mobile phone. Dialling a number, he waited while it seemed to ring forever before it was answered by a woman's voice, obviously woken from her sleep.

'Sally, sorry to wake you.'

'Tom, is that you?'

'Yes'

'How's it going? Are you alright.'

'All good. Just wanted to let you know that we have the money and that we're on track. We leave in a few hours and will see you tomorrow morning.'

'Tom, that's great news. We're very worried, and don't have any idea when the Colonel is coming.'

'Hang in there. We're all set and everything is going according to plan. Mike is going to meet us at the border and we'll call you on the radio to get coordinates for our rendezvous point.'

'That's fantastic. I can't thank you enough, Tom. We will have everyone in place and ready to go.'

'How are you coming along with the crew?'

'We should be okay, Tom, but I can't wait to get the herd moving. Good news is that Mopapi, the matriarch, has stayed in the valley, so they are not too far from the border. I'm pretty sure that, given the abundance of water and food there, she will still be there tomorrow.'

'Go back to sleep. See you soon.'

'Tom, thankyou.'

'It's what I do.'

Tom put down the phone.

'She ready?' asked Pop.

'I guess so. Can we go through that list again?'

'Sure.' Pop picked up a small notebook with a long list of items and ticked off items as he and Tom went through them. A few minutes later they were done and packing up the last of the things. A cab met them outside and whisked them to Heathrow just as the sun was coming up and before Tom knew it they were ensconced in their seats on a flight to Johannesburg. Economy Class had never felt this comfortable. Tom was oblivious to his fatigue and the crying baby two aisles down that had so many other passengers disgruntled. They were on their way and there was important work ahead … it was make or break time.

"Do you want to go over the plan Pop?' Tom asked, pouring his drink.

'Right,' said Pop, who had been staring out of the window, lost in his own thoughts.

'Okay. When we get to the border, I radio Sally for the coordinates of our meeting point in Chikangawa. I've avoided doing that ahead of time in case somebody has been tapping her phone or listening in on their radio frequency. Thabo, Marcus and Sally will all be there.'

'Great. How did the research go?'

'Well, I did some looking around and spoke to a few of my mates at Animal Relocation. It seems there has never been large herd relocation over ground. Everyone seems pretty unsure as to how the herd will react. There is a risk they will get stressed and dispurse, so we need to concentrate our efforts on Mopapi, the matriarch, and trust that by moving her the rest of the herd will follow. We have to keep them together. If any of them get anxious and bolt, chaos will ensue and things will get really dangerous, Pop.'

'I've organised ten Land Rovers from a local dealer, all in good shape – or so he says, so we should be able to contain them if we have the manpower, Son. You'll need to let Sally know that they can collect the vehicles tomorrow. My guy promises me they've been serviced and have full GPS capability. Top of the range.'

'How much did that set us back?'

'A cool hundred and eighty thousand pounds. I had to buy them.

'Great. Thanks, Pop. Sally is organising all the support kit like binoculars and dart guns and Rusty seems pretty organised with his kit. I just hope he doesn't have any problems at customs. Everything depends on him being able to sail through the checkpoint at Johannesburg International.'

'I wouldn't worry too much about that, Tom. I have a good friend there, and I'm trusting that all the right strings have been pulled. We are going to need to part with some of this cash we're carrying when we get there though. Nothing for nothing, as the saying goes.'

'Pop, you're a legend.'

'What else are we missing?'

'I'm not sure. Was going to say 'luck', but she seems to be on our side already.' Tom smiled broadly at his father as they clinked their plastic glasses.

'Whatever we don't have organised now, we'll have to do on the other side. I think we're sorted though. Thankyou, Pop. For everything.'

Pop smiled and nodded, leaning back in his seat to carry on looking out of his window.

A few minutes later he sat forward in his seat again. 'OK, so assuming you get them across, where do you deposit this herd of elephants?'

'That's Sally's department. She said she would send me the details tomorrow after confirming with some associates. A game park in the area has just been fenced, and she seemed to think it would be perfect.'

'And transport there?'

'We have rented twenty-six low-bed container trucks and fifty-two containers with all the relevant trimmings, including food for the passage. They're all en route to the area as we speak, and should be there by tomorrow night.'

'You are well organised, Son.

'Run's in the family, Pop. I think all those years you spent in the the army have rubbed off on me.'

Just then the pilot's voice came on in the cabin and confirmed that flight time to Johannesburg would be approximately another ten hours.

'I am sure you have all the bases covered,' Pop said reassuringly as they both sank back in their seats to get some sleep.

Chapter 9
GETTING THE HERD HOME

**05h00, Sunday 16 September – The South
African side of the south-western Zimbabwean border**

TOM STONE climbed into the Huey just before dawn. The
African sky was blood red and he wondered if it was a
bad omen. He reached into his duffle bag as the engines
roared and repeated the desitnation coordinates to the pilot.

'Mike, make it as fast as we can. Their lives depend on it.'

News was that the Chikangawa herd of elephants were going
to be massacred soon, maybe even today. The government had
been expropriating the sanctuary that they called home for the
last sixty years and today no farm or game reserve was safe in
the new Zimbabwe. Over the last few months, thousands of
wild animals had been slaughtered, some for their skins and
meat, others just for the sport. Farms lay in ruin as the economy
crumbled under new levels of inflation.

The helicopter revved up to speed and in a haze of white dust
rose into the dawn sky.

'How long?' Tom asked.

The pilot checked his readings. 'Maybe fifty minutes, if we
cruise.'

'The team should meet us there, how long can you give us air
support?' Tom glanced anxiously at Mike.

66

'As long as the fuel lasts. Should be able to help until dusk, given a few refuels.'

'Thanks Mike, that should do it. I hope.'

Tom and Mike had been friends for a long time, having both grown up in Africa. They had fought many battles together and today were going into battle once again. Today they were up against a war veteran and his henchmen, a situation Tom and Mike had had experience of before. Old captains of freedom who became twisted were a particularly dangerous lot, and Tom and Mike knew that things today could go either way. These guys were power tripping, trigger-happy and without conscience or remorse ... exactly the reason why Tom was not prepared to let Moroge get away with the destruction of the herd..

The dawn sky was lightening as the two friends embarked on another journey together, and the spirit of Africa embraced them both. Tom, who had been away from the bush for a long time, turned and smiled to his friend.

'A great welcome home, hey buddy?'

Mike laughed.

'Only you, my friend, could make this a homecoming.'

Tom checked his radio and adjusted to his team's frequency.

'GoodAir to Ground. Come in, Ground.'

Across the crackling line came a familiar voice.

'Ground receiving loud and clear, what is your ETA? Over.'

'Rise and shine, Thabo. We should be there before eight. Are we ready to rock n roll? Over.'

'For sure, Tom. We are ready. Vehicles packed, tanks full, any news on where the herd is? Over.'

'We think they are close to the border. At least we damn well hope they are. Over.'

'Did my special packages arrive from Hwange? Over.'

'Yes, Tom. Everything is here. Over.'

'Great. See you soon. We'll be taking a route over the southern hills to see if we can find our friends. Over and out.'

Flying east, Mike guided the Huey across the open flatlands, flying as low as he could. They were breaking a few international regulations by crossing the border unannounced. Ahead there rose between them and the dawning sun the Halangwi hills which ran for about a hundred kilometres to the north.

'Lets find our friends.' Tom leaned over to the RF kit and switched on the receiver. A single beep sounded and a directional readout indicated the direction from which the signal was received. Mike adjusted the controls and the Huey banked so that the signal was coming from directly ahead.

As they flew the beeping became more rapid and just as they cleared the first of the Halangwi hills, Tom saw the herd, walking out from a swamp side thicket onto the open sand.

This was what Tom had been waiting for. In a moment all the fatigue of a restless night on the plane and the worry of the last few days dissipated, leaving him with an incredible joy at the sight of these magnificent beasts in the African bush – and a firm resolve of what had to be done. There was no going back. The thought of anybody threatening the herd made his blood boil and gave him an instant, tight heaviness on his chest. He was prepared to risk his life for this.

'Good morning. all.' Tom said through a smile before becoming serious again and consulting his maps..

'This is good,' Tom shouted across to Mike. 'They're about thirty kilometres from the nearest border crossing, which means that if we get going we can be home and dry by tomorrow morning.'

'Beers are on me if we're home and dry by tomorrow, Tom.' Mike said jokingly as he surveyed the terrain. He was in the zone, focused on the flying, and in his element.

The herd of two hundred and twenty-three elephants drew closely together as the Huey drew nearer. The herd was made up of over thirty families, but family boundaries always broke down in the face of danger, and the majestic animals huddled together to face the noisy helicopter.

Mike and Tom had spent many months with these elephants. Mike had recently produced a documentary about poaching and they had focused on this herd because it had been successfully protected by a dedicated team of rangers who were amongst the best in the world at anti-poaching and animal protection manouevres. They had devised many strategies for large conservation areas, and had worked closely with local communities to make it possible to prevent poaching activities. Unfortunately, a year ago, this elite group had been disbanded, as the government claimed it was not cost effective. In the months that had passed since, more and more elephant had been slaughtered for ivory.

'Look at old Long Ears. They were not joking about her angel wing ears'

Mike was pointing at the far end of the herd. Mopape was one of the largest females ever recorded. Her unusually long ears made her an especially imposing figure as she moved between the herd, clearly nervous of what the helicopter represented,

'Are we going to try to reign in any of the bulls?' asked Mike.

'I doubt we'll have the time. If we see any close by, we should try and pull them in together, but it will be up to you my friend.'

'Will do what I can.'

'Well, at least we know where they are. Let's go rendezvous with the team.'

Mike pulled back on the controls and the Huey banked sharply, leaving the herd behind them as they flew due east into the morning sun.

05h01, Sunday 16 September –
The main entrance to Chikangawa

Colonel Moroge stood at the main gated entrance to Chikangawa in full battle regalia with maroon beret and a chest of ribbons. His stern face stared out into the bush, and the rising sun cast a large shadow across the white-sand road.

The gate, which was made from large trunks of local ironwood, had been locked after the land had been expropriated, as per government instructions.

'Mamabe, come here!' he shouted.

A short soldier ran from behind a green jeep.

'Sir!' he saluted and stood to attention.

'Where are the others?'

'They are on their way, Sir, fifteen minutes'

'I want to be finished with this place, I want to go back to Harare by tomorrow night, so get on the radio and make sure they are coming.'

'Yes, Sir.'

Moroge was fifty-seven years old, but was feeling much older. He was now a relic, bitter from being overlooked by his leadership and resentful of everything the white man had put him and his family through. In his mind he was still a freedom fighter, but he had lost every sense of what was right and important and now only wanted pay-back for his years of struggle.

Mamabe was a small man, a young officer who had been given the hard task of looking after a living legend in the military.

'Where is the radio?' barked Moroge.

'Here, Sir'

'Mamabe, find out where your troops are?'

Mamabe lifted the radio to his mouth and called out a few commands

A voice crackled over the radio. 'On our way, Sir. The roads are very bad and we have had some fuel problems.'

'Mamabe, I do not care, we need to move today, our scouts have spotted the animals and the transport trucks are coming in the morning. We must have that ivory cut and piled by the morning, tell your men ot hurry.'

'Yes, Sir.' Mamabe was sweating and with a shaky hand shouted into the radio.

'They are going to move faster Sir' Mamabe stood at attention waiting for the Colonel to respond.

'How many men are there with you?'

'Fifty, Sir.'

'Good, that should be enough.'

The Colonel put his hand on his Rossi 45. He felt contempt for this place rising in him. A place dedicated to white tourists, white colonialism, white domination. Even after years of so-called freedom, he still felt like he was being dictated to by the white man. Old bitterness welled up inside him and he spat at the ground.

05h52 – Southern Chikangawa

Mike brought the Huey in low and landed it near a line of Land Rovers.

Thabo came across to meet them and Tom handed him a few stainless-steel cases before jumping down to ground.

'Some gifts from the guys overseas,' Mike shouted over the din of the helicopter.

Thabo gave Tom a big bear hug and they smiled at each other. It had been some time since they were last together, and Thabo was very happy to see Tom.

They made their way to a make-shift working area under a large Baobab tree, where the bonnet of a Land Rover served as a table and boxes were being used as chairs. Laid out across the bonnet was a map of the area and the keys to the eleven Landrovers that had been assembled.

The team were all there waiting for Tom, busying themselves with last-minute preparations. The camp was a hive of activity.

Out from the back of the closest Land Rover came Doctor Sally Allan, her hair tied back to show up her delicate, freckled skin.

Tom felt a rush of joy at seeing her and walked over.

'Hello, Sally.' he said as they hugged. 'How are things going? You guys look pretty organised.'

'Thanks, Tom. Good and bad, I suppose. Better now that you are here.' she held lightly onto his arm.

Tom leaned over and gave her a kiss on the cheek.

'Here are the tranquillisers you asked for. Should be enough.' Tom handed her a silver box with a hundred small bottles of Sodium thiopental.

'That should do just fine,' she said as she transferred the anaesthetic into her backpack.

'Are you ready for the onslaught?' asked Tom, cautiously.

'It's long overdue, Tom. We are declaring war on the Colonel, though. If we succeed he will make life very difficult for us and everybody who helped us. Or worse.'

Sally looked out across the bush.

'How do they look?' she asked.

'The herd is fine, and they are on the right side. If we can move quickly we can be well underway before the Colonel gets wind of our activity.'

'Well, let's do it.' Sally gave a nod and signalled to the crew to gather, briefly introducing Tom to everyone before he took over as leader of the operation. Tom recognised a few faces from when he and Mike had worked here at Chikangawa, but there was no time for niceties.

'Good morning, everyone. I would like to thank you all for everything you've done at such short notice. As you know, this is no easy task. Even if we didn't have the time pressures and the possible interference from the Colonel, we would still be facing an upward battle. Our objective is simple, get the herd across the border before dawn tomorrow, and if the Colonel finds them, and us, to protect the herd however we can.

'We have over two hundred elephants to relocate today, and nothing like this has ever been attempted before, anywhere. You all have great experience in various areas and we're going to need every ounce of your skill and commitment to make this work.

Lastly, I have no doubt that the Colonel and his crew will do everything in their power to stop us, so watch your back and stay safe. We do have a few advantages; we have each other and the skills that each one of you has to get the job done, and we also have some pretty awesome kit. What we don't have is their firepower. I do not want any confrontation, I do not want to lose anyone out there, so let's try to avoid them as much as we can. Team leaders?'

At this four people stepped forward, all very close colleagues of Thabo's, people who had served in anti-poaching units, people who knew Chikangawa well and were determined to stop this evil. They were all Zimbaweans who had tried to make some contribution through the normal channels, but had failed to win government support. Instead they found themselves blacklisted, with potential jail sentences pending. They had had enough of the regime and the politics, and now it was time to hit back.

Tom explained that the Land Rovers would drive directly to the valley entrance. Mike and the Huey would drive the herd to the south, where, once out of the valley, the Land Rovers could drive the herd on a direct course to the South African border. The border was fenced, but once the herd was close a team on the South African side would cut an entrance through. Tom went into detail with the team on checkpoints and the specific SatNav points that each Landrover would programme into their GPS systems.

'Any luck with support from the South African authorities, Tom?' asked Thabo.

'Sorry, my friend, the best we got was that they are prepared to turn a blind eye. And that was only after a large quantity of money changed hands. We do have a team of friends and conservationists waiting at Itaga though. They will deal with the legalities and take care of the herd from there.'

'We have paid off the border unit and the patrol heads, and have a window of 20 hours to get through. They're having an equipment check today and the patrol team will be doing routine maintenance, so they should be in camp when we hope to cross and the run into South Africa should be clear. Once through, we have a capture facility about three kilometres in from the border, where there are enough trucks to load the herd and transport it to Itaga. We will have to do a night transfer to Itaga, but the South African crew will provide support once we're there.'

Tom looked around at the group of concerned faces. They were ready to move.

'Right, let's move. Everyone stay alert, stay on your radio, don't lose sight of the herd once we're with them and once they start keep them moving. I'll be on the ground until we get the herd moving, at which point I will take to the air with Mike to keep an eye on our other friends.'

Just as the group was dispersing another familiar face appeared from behind one of the Land Rovers.

'Rusty, good to see you.'

'You too, Tom. All set?'

'I was going to ask you the same thing.'

'Yup, the five green Land Rovers all have smokers attached, the buttons are on the dashes. The smokers should last for around 20 minutes each, and the smoke levels should be thick, especially with this dry air.'

'Sounds good, anything else?'

'Yup, a few tricks, but lets keep that a surprise. I have covered what needs to be done with the team leaders.' Rusty handed Thabo a control box.

'Your box of tricks. The blue button is for the smoker and the red is for the cherry bombs, which will sound like gun fire. Last but not least are the two black buttons, which are the surprise, should we get in a pickle. They should buy us a bit of time.' Rusty looked well satisfied with his work.

'So what does it do, buddy?' asked Thabo.

'All you have to do, my friends, is push that button when you are in a pinch. But for it to work properly, I must keep it a secret.'

'Surely we have to know how this thing is going to work?' Thabo asked again, this time giving Rusty a stern look. There was enough potential for surprise in the equation.

'Just kidding, Thabs. The left black button will trigger the roofrack boxes, which will detach themselves, so if you're moving they will fall behind the vehicle. By pushing the right button, they will ignite, and in this bush should start a small fire. There is a pretty large pack of pyro in each container, so it should make the enemy stop for a while.'

'Awesome, thanks Rusty,' said Tom, now impatient to get going. 'You guys all know what to do. Good luck out there.'

Thabo shouted some additional instructions to the team as they entered their vehicles. Each Land Rover had two people in it; one to drive and one to navigate and use the radio. The five green landrovers would drive behind the six white, which were to be used as chase vehicles. Each white Land Rover was specially kitted with bull bar, cages around the lights and front windscreens, and an additional hooter attached to the hood. The chase vehicles also had massive spotlights on the roof so that they could work effectively at night.

The final vehicle was a Unimog, with water tank, food supplies and medical equipment.

Other than their own personal weapons, the team had very little firepower, choosing rather to avoid where possible any engagements with the enemy.

Tom joined Thabo in the lead vehicle and they drove out from under the big tree into the open bush. There were no roads in this section of Chikangawa, so they would have to drive fairly slowly through the thick bushveld.

Once through the lower section they would come out onto the open plains that would run almost to the border, but there was however one more obstacle. A kilometre or so from the border there was thick mopane veld, which would make driving in Land Rovers difficult unless they got lucky, or with Mike's help found a way through.

Tom drove a hundred or so meters ahead of the rest, and a large dust trail rose behind him. A soft southwesterly wind was blowing and he hoped that the dust trail would not give away their position too early. Maybe they would be lucky and the Colonel wouldn't make a move until later in the day.

The convoy of vehicles moved slowly through the thick bush Thabo gripped his radio in his hand as he was shaken about on the rough terrain.

'Radio test, everyone who can hear me sound off. Over.'

'Green one, receiving.'

'Green two, receiving.'

As each responded in turn so Tom's thoughts wandered to how these events had all come to pass. He had heard about the Zimbabwe elephant massacres while in London, which had been especially difficult because the reports were from a place he had once called home, a place where he knew the people and a place where he had found shelter from the world. Chikangawa was

Eden, and Eden it was. Wealthy colonialists had set it up as a private game reserve in the 1950s and even after Zimbabwe's independence it had been the epitome of the conservation effort. For years it had remained a private game reserve, providing an intimate experience of both wild sanctuary and the Matabele way of life. The reserve had boasted ten rustic camps and accommodation in two Matabele villages, making it one of the most unique tourist attractions around. A large number of the Matabele villagers also made their living from the reserve and many became passionate about the area, as the land next to the reserve had been donated to the villagers for agricultural use.

The route Tom would take was through the open grassland, going up to the escarpment where there were sand tracks from the ranger station. This would be the fastest route.

Behind the team, Mike waited inside the cockpit of the Huey for word from Tom to spring into action.

06h05 – Outside Chikangawa's main gate

Moroge's officers faced him at attention as he glared and shouted angrily at them for arriving late at the rendezvous location.

'Why is it I cannot get efficiency? I have been patient enough with you all, it is time for you all to start to act like soldiers. In my day when we were fighting for freedom, we had no training camps, no three meals a day, no beds, you people are spoilt and soft.'

The Colonel had sweat droplets on his forehead, which he wiped with a white handkerchief. His officers stood, not moving a muscle.

'Now, why is it taking so long? Mamabe, what do you have to say for yourself?' the Colonel shouted.

'Fuel, Sir. The troop carriers needed diesel and they had to drive to Hlungwe, but they had run dry, so they had to raid a local farmer, Sir.'

Mamabe stamped his feet together at attention again.

'You are making me very angry. Now where is the map?'

Mamabe opened a map on a nearby folding table.

'Where are these damned animals, these elephants?'

'We do not know, but the spotter plane is on the way. We should have them spotted just after midday, Sir.'

Mamabe saw it as a great honour and privilege to be serving such an esteemed military hero from their fight for freedom.

'I want to get moving, so break the locks on this gate and let's make our way in so that we are ready when those helicopters arrive.'

'Yes, Sir.'

Mamabe shouted some order and two soldiers ran to the gate with an unusually large hydraulic cutter. They broke open the thick chains and threw the gates open.

The army division made their way into the gate camp, which had once been a luxurious welcome area for international tourists but now stood derelict. Some of the doors and widows were missing and the thatch on some of the buildings had been pulled out.

The Colonel walked through the gates and looked around at a place he had once visited. As a senior member of the military, he had decided to visit with his family, but was surrounded by foreign white people. That was enough to put him off and this, finally, was his chance to put another nail in the colonial coffin.

'Get me my Jeep!' the Colonel called across to his Mamabe.

'It is time to go. Mamabe, get this group moving.'

'Yes, Sir.' Mamabe saluted and ran to a troop carrier

A plume of dust rose up into the sky as the convoy made its way from the gate camp eastwards on one of the dirt roads leading into the reserve.

08h50 – Entrance to the Tlokwe valley

Tom heard Mike on the radio, but was busy driving a difficult section of the sand road, just south of the escarpment entrance.

'Green one, come in, this is Goodair, come in green.' Mike's voice crackled over the speaker.

Thabo was on the roof, navigating a tricky section through a thick sand track. They had deflated the Land Rover's tyres to get through this short cut to the mountain road, but the thick sand was proving to be a challenge.

'Green one, come in,' Mike called again.

Tom did not want to stop to answer, but then he heard Sally respond.

'Goodair, this is green six, Green one busy learning to drive in the sand, doing well, anything you need?'

'Yes, I am about to get airborne, are you close to checkpoint?' Mike asked.

'Yes Mike, we are almost at the entrance, another thirty minutes and we should be in position,' Sally answered.

'Great, will make my way over to you. See you soon. Over and out.'

Mike powered up the Huey and, closing the door, made a final check before throttling up and taking off.

Taking a sweeping turn to the south, he flew towards the valley entrance, but something caught his eye. To the east on the horizon was a large column of dust rising from the ground. He made one more turn to check his eyesight, and it was still there. He hoped it was a dust storm, but he knew better. It may be the Colonel, and if so he was on the move far too early. He was in a position to cut them off and had the advantage of a fast-moving unit on his side.

Mike grabbed the radio.

'Goodair to Green one. Come in, Green one. Urgent news.'

Tom had just come to the end of a gruelling hour of sand driving, and was having a drink of water. Behind him the others were all battling through the sandy tracks

'Hi, Mike. What's up?'

'It looks like the Colonel is on the move, Tom, and he is not that far away.'

Tom nearly dropped his water bottle.

'Say again, Mike?'

'There is a large dust column just past the main gate complex. If it is him, he is less than four hours away.'

Tom looked at his watch, and glanced over to Thabo.

'We are going to have to move into top gear,' Tom said.

'We are ready, Tom. Let's go for it.'

'Mike.' Tom's voice was firm. 'Get here as quickly as you can and pick me up. Let's go and get our friends, we need to get the herd moving. We also need to determine whether or not the Colonel is coming for us, how fast, and how many team members he has. Green two, go up to the top of Leopard Rock and use your scope to give us as much information as you can. You should be able to get to the top by around 09h30. Take the rear road, so that your climb is short. Go, go, go!' he shouted into the radio.

Tom jumped down from the Land Rover and packed a bag with some binoculars, a small mobile GPS and some food and water. Just as he finished packing, another Land Rover pulled up behind his and Sally got out.

'Game's on,' she said, looking concerned.

'Like old times,' Mike said with a wink.

Sally thought about the first time she had met Tom. It was in this reserve, many years ago. She had caught him smuggling cheetah into the park, having stolen them from farmers who had trapped them on nearby farms. She had had to deal with poachers and politicians, but never with anyone who was willing to stretch and break the rules to such an extent to make ends meet in the very delicate world of conservation. She liked his strength and determination, but mostly she admired how he never negotiated; Tom did what had to be done, and he did it really well.

'You want to come with us?' Tom asked

'You got space?'

'We'll squeeze you in. It may be better for you to be more mobile, though. Pack all your kit.'

By the time Sally had finished packing, Mike's helicopter could be heard flying closer.

Tom and Sally carried all their kit up to a clearing and signalled Mike to come in for a dusty landing. Mike did not even throttle back, but waited for all the kit and Sally and Tom to jump in and immediately took off again, leaving the rest of their crew, who had just arrived at the scene, eating dust.

'The helicopter entered the valley and flew north to the river, following it north-east to a series of swamplands. The sun was now high in the sky, but they were making good time in terms of their original plan.

A few minutes into the flight they saw the herd.

Grazing in a thicket of marsh reeds, over two hundred of the magnificent animals looked up to see what the noise was. Mopapi reacted to the noise by running out and putting herself between the herd and the Huey, but the herd was relaxed, which was not what Tom wanted.

'Now to get them running!' Tom shouted as he opened a pack of cherry bombs and started to arm them with small fuses.

'Mike, bring me round to the north. Let's see if we can get them to run south.' Tom pointed to a small cluster of trees.

Mike nodded and flew sideways until the herd was south of them. Sally had armed herself with a small hand-held flare and when Tom gave her the nod she lit it.

'Lets get them moving.' Tom held five cherry bombs with attached fuses and Sally lit them one by one before Tom threw them out of the window and they exploded with deafening sound, one by one.

All the elephants jumped at the first blast, and by the time the fifth blew they were in full flight southwards, with Mopapi leading the way. They had gathered together, protecting the calves of the herd between their large bodies.

Their natural behaviour would be to run for two or three hundred metres and then to turn around and see if they were still under threat. The idea was to keep them moving though, and not to let them get separated in the panic of it all.

Mike flew the Huey low to the ground and came in close on their heels. Just then Mopapi suddenly turned and stopped allowing the rest of the herd to run past her down the riverbed. She was making a stand.

'Mike, get us close. We need to give her a bit of a fright; she's a little too confident today.'

Tom knew that Mopapi was going to be a challenge and he wanted to take the upper hand. If they lost control of the matriarch now the battle would be lost before they had even begun.

Tom attached another battery of fuses and Sally lit them quickly before they were thrown to the ground. The five seemed to go off almost immediately, giving the herd even more speed, but Mopapi stood her ground.

'Shit! We're going to have to force her,' said Tom. He had known that she wasn't just going to follow instuctions.

Tom thought that maybe the sound of the cherry bombs was a bit like thunder and just wasn't frightening enough. She had been shot before, though, so she would be more likely to respond to the sound of gunfire.

'Mike, where is the rifle?'

'Back of the seat, behind you. It's loaded, so be careful.'

Tom pulled out the 30 odd 6 hunting rifle from its bag, and after giving it a quick once over he shouldered the butt and aimed out of the open door down towards the ground, firing twice at the ground just next to where Mopapi stood.

Still she stood her ground, flapping her ears and waving her trunk as if to scare off these noisy intruders.

'God damn it, she is tough. I have another idea, Mike. Fly off a hundred meters and drop me next to that big trunk. I'm thinking that maybe she'll remember poachers on foot. Fly off behind me so that she can not hear too much chopper noise.'

'Will do, Tom. Be careful down there. You know she has killed before.'

'Yes, but she is also very wary of a man with a gun. It's worth a try.'

Mike flew in low and let Tom out before flying up the valley and coming down to land.

Tom looked down the riverbed.

Mopapi was looking back and flapping her ears, showing her aggravation at this unwanted interruption to her herd's otherwise peaceful day. Behind her the herd had halted and were looking up the riverbed in his direction. She was standing in an open riverbed about fifty metres away from Tom, who only had the protection of a tree trunk behind him. If anything went wrong, this would be all the protection he would have. Elephants do not often run a man down, but Mopapi had done so and it had been rumoured she had done it more than once.

Tom walked about five paces, kneeled down and aimed the rifle at a broken tree to Mopapi's left. She was flapping her ears more vigorously now and waving her trunk from left to right. And then, with an almighty trumpet, she charged.

Tom had little time, but decided to fire twice. The shots echoed off the walls of the valley and Mopapi stopped. Tom, expecting a full charge, had already run the distance to the large tree trunk, but on turning could see Mopapi standing, flapping her ears. The herd in the background also seemed to be standing still.

Tom, hoping that he could get Mopapi to flee south, kneeled again and fired a volley of five shots to her left. Mopapi ignored the volley at first, but then gave out a low droning call before turning and running south past the herd, which pulled in behind her. Their padded feet gave off a soft rumbling as the entire herd began running south, even the smallest falling in behind their mothers at speed.

Tom was stupefied, wondering if Mopapi somehow knew what they were trying to do. But that was impossible. Wasn't it? There was no way she could know. So why was it so easy? Tom realised he would never know, but thanked the gods for this good fortune. He knew it would be very difficult to get Mopapi to move south, and hoped that things would continue to run in his team's favour.

Signalling Mike with thumbs up, he walked into the clearing where he was swooped up. Wrapping his arm around the handrail, he stood on the footrail while they flew in behind the herd.

Flying low, Tom realised just how many elephant there were. The entire herd had joined in the run and there was a cloud of dust rising behind them. Maybe Mopapi just wanted to get them out of the valley, but whatever the reason, this was good fortune for the team. The Land Rovers would represent a far greater threat, especially with their blaring horns and flashing lights. It was a great start.

Just then the radio crackled to life.

'Goodair, this is Green two. We are at the view point and have some details for you. Over.'

'Great effort, guys. That's good going. What can you see?' Mike asked.

'Not good news. It is definitely the Colonel and it seems as though he has brought a small army with him. Must be about ten troop carriers, twelve transport trucks and three armoured cars. The Colonel's Jeep is at the front. The good news is that he does not seem to be in a very big hurry, not sure why, but they are travelling west on the central road at only about thirty kilometres an hour.'

'Is there any air support?' asked Tom.

'Not that we can see. Would you like us to stay perched here? Over.'

'Yes, but just for the next hour, then give us another update. We are on our way, should be out of the valley before midday.'

Tom stayed on the radio.

'Goodair to all Green units, we are moving. The Angel has decided to lead her herd south, lucky for us. Get in position. They are moving steadily and should be there within forty minutes. We will need to steer them as planned, and I think if Rusty can give them a bit of a push with some tricks, all the better.'

'Goodair, this is Green two. We are already in position and Rusty is working his magic, see you shortly. Over.'

Tom felt that maybe fate was on their side, but experience had taught him that the best intentions of the bravest and most virtuous people were often the target of unfortunate events. He hoped that this would be their day though.

Even with this feeling of good fortune, Tom was anxious. The news about the Colonel was bad. Tom had never met the man, but knew from the stories he had heard that this man was without conscience or remorse and was capable of the greatest atrocities against man and animal alike. Tom was now worried that if there was a confrontation, people could be killed, and this was never the plan.

10h08 – Deep in the Chikangawa bush

The Colonel called the division to a halt and climbed out of his Jeep, signalling for Mamabe to set up a table and chairs under a nearby tree. The sun was beating down and the Colonel's brow was beaded with sweat.

Once the table and chairs were set up, the Colonel went and reclined in a chair under the cooler shade of the trees and was served up some cold water, tea and cake. The Colonel had a sweet tooth and as a rule always had a good rich chocolate cake on hand. He felt this was a small luxury for what he saw as a lifetime of service.

'Mamabe, my lieutenants!' The Colonel was still in a bad mood. Maybe from being passed over again for a senior government post, maybe from his debt, maybe from his frozen assets.

The soldiers all came running and stood at attention in front of the table.

'Where are those vermin?'

'Sir, we are still waiting for the spotter plane. It has been delayed at the local airport.'

'It is after midday and we are still waiting. Where is this plane, and why not a helicopter? At least they could pick me up!'

'Sorry, Sir, but command would not let us use any of the helicopters. Not for an unauthorised operation, Sir,' Mamabe answered.

'As I said earlier, this is for the Minister!' The Colonel's voice was rising again. Why did he have to explain himself to these young troops who never had to fight for their country or for their freedom? He thought his story a good one, as the minister was revered and they would not question him about this again.

Just then, one of the radio personnel pulled off his headphones and called the Colonel's adjutant over. Mamabe smiled and turned to the Colonel.

'Sir, we have something. There is a lot of dust at the entrance to the Tlokwe valley. It looks like it may be the herd. Nothing else would make that much dust, and Jonas was somewhere near there a few days ago.

'Alright, Mamabe. Forget the plane. Let's drive there right away and find these damned animals.'

10h36 – Bottom of the Tlokwe Valley

At a steady pace, the elephants had made it to the entrance of the valley and had come to a stop slightly west of the Land Rover convoy. Mike needed to refuel so they had turned back to the camp. Tom also wanted to check the route. At least the herd was out of the valley and the open terrain would make life a little easier now, should the herd decide to turn back on their tracks.

'Goodair to Green one to six, we are almost back at camp. What are your positions?'

'Green One to Goodair, we have the herd in sight and we have closed the door on the valley. Only problem is that they have stopped moving. I think they are a little stressed after the chase.'

'Leave them to rest until we get back to you, but don't let them go back on their tracks.'

'Will do, Tom. See you in fifteen.'

Mike landed the Huey at base camp and as the rotors on the helicopter slowed, Tom opened the doors and ran through the dust swirl to the meeting area. He wanted to check the more detailed map with Mike, even though they had been over it a hundred times. Some old aerial photos showed some old tracks that had been made by hunters and game rangers. These would make passage a little easier for the ground team, but getting the herd to follow a track was almost impossible.

Mike signalled the fuel team and they drove a modified Land Rover to the chopper, pumping enough fuel into it to last another two hours.

Mike and Tom stood at the map, considering their options.

'It looks like we could try to get them to this spot here. We can then look for a way through the thick Mopani forest to the border.'

'Looks like a good route, fairly flat except for this short rocky outcrop. We will have to go around this, as the herd will not be able to get through, neither will the Landy's.'

'I think we should aim for north of the outcrop, to this landmark.' Tom pointed to a small hill of exposed rock which could be seen from around five kilometres, giving the team something to aim for.

'Lets do it then.'

Mike and Tom ran back to the chopper and Mike throttled up once again, rising out of the dust and turning north again to rejoin the team.

11h12 – North East from the Tlokwe Valley

The colonel could see the dust rising from the valley entrance through his binoculars.

'Mamabe, how far are we from there?'

'One hour, Sir. Our Unimogs can follow the trail right up to the entrance.'

'Good, let's keep them moving!

The convoy moved slowly through the soft sand.

11h38 – Buzzing the convoy

'Green two to Goodair. We have more news. Come in. Over.'

'Go ahead Green two,' Mike answered.

'The convoy is en route, travelling at speed. We estimate the Colonel will be at the herd's current location within the hour.'

Tom looked at Mike.

'Maybe we should fly over them and take a look, find out what we are facing?' asked Mike.

'They are en route, so there is no point in hiding, and it will give us a better idea of what we are facing. Let's do it.'

'Rusty, come in.'

'Yes, Tom, reading you loud and clear.'

'We need you to work your magic and get the herd moving again. For the moment due west will do.'

'Will give them some incentive, Tom.'

'Good stuff.'

'Let's go and have a look, Mike.'

Mike turned the helicopter southeast and made for the dust plumes in the distance, leaving the team to get the herd moving again. The radio crackled with team instructions from Thabo and Rusty. Behind them small explosives shattered the morning silence, and followed by revving, hooting and flashing lights. The herd started moving once again, this time swinging west into the flat land that lay between them and the border.

Mike flew low, just meters above the flat bushveld. The day was warming up and Tom could feel the warm air on his face coming in through the ventilation duct. The horizon shimmered in the growing heat. Mike aimed the Huey directly towards the dust cloud that seemed to be constantly expanding.

'Shit, that cloud looks like its being made by an entire convoy, Mike. I really hope that they are not expecting us. They seem to be in a hurry and are driving on our tracks. Get us close and pull up so that we can take a closer look.'

'Will do. What happends if they shoot at us though?'

'Keep it brief. We'll make the pass a quick one. Do one of those flip manoeuvres you're famous for. That way we get a good look and they don't get a chance to hit us.'

'It's risky, Tom. But I guess we need to know what we're up against.'

The Huey roared over the ground, the dust cloud growing ever bigger in front of them.

Mike waited until he was right up to the cloud before he pushed the throttle to its maximum and pulled the Huey up into the sky. Flying almost directly skyward, Mike then turned the chopper back to face the ground and flying vertically towards the convoy, he gave Tom a complete view of what they were facing. They both grimaced.

'Shit, that's a lot of convoy.'

There was a line of around twenty vehicles; a few armoured cars and what looked like off-road transport trucks. Of even greater concern at the front was a jeep followed by two troop carriers bursting with soldiers wearing camouflage uniforms and holding what looked like automatic weapons.

. 'Our lucky start has just ended,' Tom said under his breath as he turned to Mike who was levelling the chopper out as it neared the ground.

'Want another look?' asked Mike.

'No thanks, I think I've seen enough.'

'Shit, they look like they mean business.'

'We're outnumbered and a little outgunned.'

'How far are they from the herd?'

'Not more than an hour at their current pace'

'We need to get back. Rusty is going to have to rig something big to buy us some time.

The Colonel looked up at the helicopter which was roaring off westward.

'Mamabe, was that our air support? It looked civilian.'

'No sir, we were hoping for a spotter plane. It must be the park chopper, or somebody else.'

'Mamabe, I think there is more to it than that. I have never seen a chopper here, and Jonas never spoke of one. Are we getting air support or not?'

'Still no confirmation, Sir.'

'Well I want to get to the herd as soon as possible. Send the faster vehicles ahead, and make sure they are armed. If anyone gets in our way, they will pay with their lives.'

The Colonel lifted his binoculars and surveyed the valley foothills where he saw a small puff of grey smoke.

'There is something going on here, Mamabe, and I hold you responsible for all of this mess. No air support, helicopters, and some activity in the valley. If Jonas's friends have stolen some of my ivory, you will feel the pain.'

Mamabe's face showed signs of a man under pressure. Beads of sweat covered his forehead and his eyes were red from lack of sleep and worry. Had he not prepared properly? Had he missed something? He had counted on Jonas's loyalty and that had ended unexpectedly. What else could possibly go wrong?

Just then Mamabe's radio crackled and a voice confirmed that air support had departed and was only minutes away. Mamabe gave their coordinates and turned to the Colonel to salute before running off to organise a reconnaissance team.

The Colonel wiped his face with a small towel. The time had come and his thoughts wondered into the future where he and his family were once again safe from all this, out of harm's way.

11h45 – Mike's Huey

'Goodair to Green Team, we have just buzzed our good Colonel and we're going to have to move up our schedule. We're coming in fast. How is it going with the herd?'

'Not well, the old girl does not seem too interested in running from the Landy's, but Rusty is hatching a plan.'

'We will be back in position in five minutes. Green Two, are you still at lookout?'

'Yes Goodair, we are still at lookout. will keep you posted as to the Colonel's whereabouts.'

Mike flew low and fast back towards the herd and in the distance saw the white flashes of some of Rusty's thunder claps. Rusty had created a launcher for the movie industry that shot small cardboard cylinders containing a special mix which created a flashing explosion when it hit the ground. On camera the flashes looked very realistic, but even if the cylinder landed at your feet it did nothing more than scald the skin.

The Huey flew in over the herd and Tom and Mike could see that they had scattered. The thunderous sound of the explosions had done more harm than good as members of the herd members had run in opposite directions instead of together as planned.

'Green Team, split the Landys into two groups. Thabo, take the northern side. Rusty, take the southern side. Let's try and bring the herd together again. We need them all together. I am also concerned about their stress levels. They would have run a fair distance without food or water. We need to make sure that the cross-border points have all the necessaties so that we can bring down their stress levels. If not we will go through all of this only to lose half the herd.'

The Landys repositioned themselves and slowly all the outer herd members made their way back into formation.

'Mike, bring us up the middle. Hopefully Mopapi will get the message and start moving again.'

As the chopper hovered closer to the eastern side of the herd, the Land Rover teams drove into position.

'On my signal, start hooting and flashing lights. We will buzz them from our position. Once they get going, try to keep close. The terrain is rough, but we must keep them on our planned course. Keep checking your GPS's so we can be sure we're all moving in the right direction. OK. Go, go, go!'

Mike moved the Huey closer to the first group. Mopapi was on the northern side, facing the Landys as they started their approach, lights flashing and hooting bellowing. She stood her ground. The rest of the herd ran round in circles, but without her signal to move they remained within a hundred metres of their matriarch.

Just then a four-engined plane cruised over the trees just behind the Huey. This gave Mopapi the kick-start she needed and, turning herself westward to open space where there was no obstruction, she started running again.

'What the hell is that?' Mike turned the chopper to get a better view of the passing aircraft.

'Looks military. Has a Zimbabwe registration. Do you think it's the Colonel?' Mike asked Tom.

'A half-hour ago everything was going our way, now everything is going against us.'

'Not everything, my friend. Look at the herd.'

The herd had regrouped and was moving quickly through the open veld at what looked like a good speed.

'Let's keep them moving, don't let them stop. We are going to have to get them across the border before dark. Anything less and we will be facing the Colonel, and then things may become very dangerous for us and the herd.'

'Goodair to Green Team, keep them moving. Rusty, can you pull out of the group and come with us? We are going to have to try to slow that convoy down. We need some magic.'

'Will do,' Rusty said as he pulled the Landy off the track he was following and drove into an opening where Mike flew in and landed. Rusty gathered together two large shoulder bags, which were very heavy. Carrying one at a time he loaded them on the Huey before jumping in behind Tom and Mike.

'We need to keep those troops busy for at least an hour.'

'I can help with that.' Rusty smiled back.

'We will have to set up somewhere in front of them, but they seem to be cutting some of their own tracks. Is there anywhere on the map that they will have to travel over?'

'Yes, here.' Mike pointed to two small hills covered in small rocks. On either side of the hills there was a sheer wall, not more than three feet high but impossible to drive over in the type of vehicle the Colonel was using.

'They will have to pass through here as going around would add half and hour to their travel time. Assuming, of course, that they are in pursuit of us.'

'Let's go, Mike. we need to get there, set the show up and get out before we are seen,

Mike throttled up again and turned back towards the convoy that seemed ever closer to the team of friends working hard to save this herd from what awaited them.

12h00 – On to the Tlokwe Valley

The Colonel sat in the back of the lead jeep. He was being knocked around on the rough terrain and beneath his breath he was grumbling at how once again he had to be present to make an operation succeed.

Behind the Colonel a convoy of over twenty vehicles was creating a large grey cloud of swirling dust.

The track they were travelling was levelling out and in the distance they could see the base of the Tlokwe valley about five kilometres away.

Wiping his soaked head once more, the Colonel shut his eyes and looked to the future, where he had his family with him again, in a foreign land where the past could be buried and he could start again, free from the chains of this place.

Ahead of the Colonel, sitting next to the driver, Mamabe was busy on the radio. Replacing the receiver, he stood and signalled the convoy to halt.

'Sir, the spotter plane has been flying below the valley. They have the herd in sight, but there is a problem.'

'What problem, Mamabe? They have seen the herd, they must tell us where they are. What could be the problem?'

'It is not the herd, Sir? It is what is with the herd. It seems that a group of some sort is driving the herd westward. According to the pilot, they have twenty off-road vehicles and are being supported by that helicopter we saw.'

The Colonel sat up.

'Is that spotter plane armed?'

'No sir, only with flares.'

'How far ahead are our reconnaissance teams?

'They will be with the herd within an hour'

'Where are they taking the herd? There is nowhere they can go.'

'Sir, it seems to me that they may be taking them across the border'

'What, to South Africa? Mamabe, how?'

'Would you like me to alert the border authorities?'

'No, Mamabe. This is for us to take care of. I do not want that useless border patrol involved with this. And the Minister will not be happy if it turns into such a big operation. We need to shut these guys down on our own. And we need to do it now.'

'Yes, Sir. What should we do?'

'Get the plane to mark where they are with flares and get the recon units in place. I want all those involved killed. They must know who they are dealing with. No one person must be left alive. Is that clear?'

'But, Sir, that would be killing innocent people. This is not part of our plan.'

'Mamabe, do not question me. If we do it any other way we leave ourselves exposed and we will all pay the price. '

'But, Sir, we do not even know who these people are.'

'I do, Mamabe. It is that vet woman, the one Jonas spoke to, she has found some people to help her go against the Minister. We needed to get rid of her anyway. She knows too much. Her death will be at the hands of poachers and nobody will be any wiser.'

'Yes, Sir.'

12h38, Sunday 16 September – south west of the convoy

Mike brought the Huey in to land directly between the two hills covered in rocks. Between them lay the only passage for the Colonel's convoy and and this would be a good place to try to slow them down.

The rotors slowed and the dust settled. Rusty pulled the bags out and laid out ten small boxes in a row, each box about the same size as a cigarette pack with a fuse attached at the top.

'Mike, Tom, give us a hand.'

Mike and Tom had been looking at the map, but quickly moved over to Rusty.

'What can we do?'

'Attach these lengths of wire to the fuses on each charge. Make sure that they are all different lengths, we don't want them going off at the same time.'

'What are these Rusty?' Tom asked as he started to attach the first of the wires to a charge.

'They are gunshot props; give off the same sound as a gunshot. These grey boxes are single shot versions, the blue boxes are machine-gun fire. I have variable fuse lengths attached, so it should take them a good half-an-hour to figure out that there is nobody there.

'But surely they will know that nobody is shooting at them?'

'That, my friend, will be taken care of by the second bag.'

It took Mike, Rusty and Tom ten minutes to wire up all the charges.

'Now we need to find a good place for them behind each hill. We want to create a crossfire situation. We're going to have to bury the coils under the road. That will give the impression of bullets hitting the ground.' Rusty ran up the first hill with Tom and Mike behind.

They had just laid out all the charges when Tom saw two military off-road trucks come over a rise less than a kilometre away.

'Shit, they're here! I was hoping we'd have a little more time.' Tom cursed as he knelt down behind a rock.

'We won't even have time to get into the air, grunted Mike, 'they're only a few minutes away.'

Tom saw that they were driving in low range through some softer sand and they were probably about ten minutes away.

'Mike, get in the air. We'll stay down here and get set up. I think these trucks must be driving quite a distance in front of the convoy as reconnaissance. If so, we will have to let them pass. If they notice us, this little diversion will fail.'

Mike nodded and without another word ran down the hill to the chopper and started the engines..

'Rusty, lets keep low and get a good look at these guys.'

The trucks had passed through the sand faster than expected and before Mike had the Huey in the air they rounded a bend and caught sight of the chopper. In an instant they stopped the vehicles and two men dressed in camouflage jumped from the back of one of the trucks, carrying with them heavy machine guns. They both jumped up on the sides of the front vehicle, which started to drive towards the Huey.

'Okay, Mike. They have guns. Get out of here.'

'Nearly there, just need a few more revs and I'm gone.'

The trucks were only a hundred meters from the helicopter when it took off. Jumping from the trucks, the soldiers knelt on the ground and hurled a volley of shots at the Huey.

'Holy shit,' Rusty whispered from behind the rocks. 'What's up with these guys?'

'I was hoping we'd be spared this kind of firepower, but it seems I was wrong,' Tom said as he watched the Huey anxiously. That was his best friend in there.

The Huey climbed quickly but Tom could see that the windscreen had been hit. Mike was a great pilot and had flown in war conditions. In reaction to the shots, he banked the Huey away from the direction of fire and at full throttle thundered behind the western hill.

'Mike, are you hit?' Tom called on the radio.

The shots were sparking off the chopper's undercarriage and ricocheting off in whistles and cracks.

Mike's voice came over the two-way radio.

'For fuck's sake, that was too close Feel like I'm back in the airforce again.

'Are you okay? How is the chopper?'

Tom was concerned for his friend, and also for the most important piece of equipment they had. The operation was over if the chopper was grounded.

I'm good, Tom. Seems it may just be my windscreen that's damaged. Visibility a little impaired, but otherwise it seems we may be okay. I took a few shots underneath though, and I'll need to properly assess the damage. Going to land a few kilometres north and have a look. Keep your heads down, these guys mean business.'

Tom and Rusty could hear the engines of the Huey roaring behind the hills. They remained crouched behind the rocks, their eyes trained on the two trucks below. The commander got out from the leading truck and spoke, waving his arms at the two soldiers who had fired on the helicopter. They listened intently and then ran behind the truck and climbed inside.

'I hope they don't stick around. I wonder how far behind the other convoy members are.'

'I hope far back enough so that we can get properly set up.'

The commander of the leading truck shouted at the rear vehicle and six troops jumped from inside the canvas covering, armed with the same guns as the other two. After the commander shouted a few orders they made their way cautiously down the road and around the hills, looking for anything or anyone that had been left behind by the chopper.

They made their way up the road about a hundred metres and then, turning back, split up. Four made their way up the eastern slope and four up the western slope. If they came up high enough they would find Tom and Rusty who were behind a broad outcrop but would be easily seen on the horizon if they moved.

Down below the commander was on the radio.

'Shit, they are getting close. You armed, Rusty?'

'Nope mate, just my knife. Any ideas?'

'Sit tight, we may get lucky. If not, we're busted.'

As the one group of four soldiers walked up to the first of the rocks shielding Tom and Rusty, the Commander suddenly shouted for them to return to the trucks. They were just a few metres from seeing the bags of explosive charges.

'Phew! That was close,' Tom sighed after the soldiers had climbed back into their trucks.

'Mike, come in.' Tom called on the radio.

'Yes, Tom, I hear you.'

'Looks like they are moving again. We should be ready for pick-up in about twenty minutes. How is the chopper?'

'Not too bad. Took a hit on one of the electric fuse boxes, but the damage is minimal. Should be easy to repair. Nothing critical.'

The trucks were moving northwards over the soft sand. Once they had disappeared over the horizon Tom and Rusty walked down to the road again and quickly dealt with the small explosive boxes, burying sheets of them a few inches under the sand so that their detonation would create the effect of bullets hitting the sand.

'What's next, Rusty?' asked Tom.

'Last but not least, we have the infrared control switch. Shouldn't take more than a few minutes to wire up. This little thing will make it all work like a symphony.' Rusty showed Tom a black box covered with switches.

'The box sends each charge a signal to ignite so that the sand jumps in tandem with the detonation of the gunfire charges. We just need to synchronise the whole thing so that it goes off at the right time when the convoy is in the right place.'

Rusty rolled out a three-metre length of flat rubber matting, which had two wires at the end.

'What's that, Rust?'

'Pressure pad to arm the fuses, then an infrared to set them off. We'll place them about twenty metres apart, hopefully to avoid any birds or animals setting off the charges.'

'Rusty, you think of everything.'

'Well don't thank me yet. If we were doing a movie this would take me three days to set up. I'm not sure an hour will do it justice.'

Once finished, Tom and Rusty covered up their tracks by raking over the sand with some branches of a thorn tree.

Finally, Rusty attached a small battery pack to the control switch and turned it on. 'Ready to rumble,' he announced with a smile and buried the box just under the ground, patting the soil and walking backwards to inspect his work.

'How do we know whether it has gone off?' asked Tom.

'We will be able to hear it all, in stereo, my friend. The control switch also has a microphone and I have programmed it to broadcast to a specific frequency, as long as we are less than twenty kilo's away, we should be able to hear everything.'

Just then the sound of Mike's chopper filled the air. Tom and Rusty made their way to the same open patch where Mike had landed previously.

'Welcome back, boys.' Mike's smiling face greeted them as they opened the door.

'How did everything go?'

'So far, so good. What about the trucks?'

'They're moving pretty fast. We had better think of a way to slow them down.'

'How is the herd doing?'

'Still moving, but they have slowed. I think the ordeal is making them tired, and stressed. They haven't fed today.

'They can feed when they are safe.' Tom grimaced. 'Where are they?'

'Slipping a bit north, but still on track to get to the border in the next three hours.'

The Huey climbed and turned back towards the herd.

'Mike, take us to the trucks. We need to see where they are and then track what lies in front of them. Rusty, any ideas?'

'We can take out a tyre or two, but the charges are dangerous. I have four high-powered explosives, which should take one or two tyres off.'

'We have to slow them down or, better yet, stop them altogether.'

'All we need is two pressure pads to arm the charges or a remote control, if we set them off ourselves.'

'Mike?'

'I'm on it.'

'Goodair to Green Team, report in please. What is your progress?'

Sally came in.

'We are doing well, making good progress, if not moving a little more to the north than hoped. Seems Mopapi wants to follow a trail up towards an old water point. Good news is that that water point is close to the border and full enough for all of them to drink a little before we move on.'

'Great, Sal. Keep them moving.'

'What news of the Colonel, Tom?'

'We are only just ahead of them. We ran into some of his men and the chopper took some fire, but thanks to Mike's quick thinking the damage is minor. We can't let that happen again though, so Rusty has been putting up some diversions. We have one more to set and then we'll join you. But keep that herd moving. Don't stop. We still need to reach the border within the next three hours.'

'Wer'e on track, Tom. Keep safe. Over and out.' Sally signed off.

Mike flew very low as fast as the terrain would allow over the open savannah. Following the truck's tracks, they quickly caught up with the vehicles still struggling to make their way through the soft sand.

Keeping it low and fast, Mike came up behind them before they had time to register the chopper's presence or react to it. The Huey shot over the trucks, whose occupants looked up in surprise. Even with their commander yelling 'Fire, fire!' they were too slow as the Huey had already passed them by.

Now to get some height to see which way they were going.

13h28

The two diesel trucks were very comfortable in off-road conditions. Tailor-made for combat in the African bush, they had high axels and extremely powerful engines that drove a 'built-for–the-kill' four-wheel drive system. These vehicles were one of the fastest of their kind and could cover ground quickly over rough terrain. The one thing they did not like was big rocks. They were made to be fast in open sand, but slowed when moving over bigger obstacles. If they attempted to drive more quickly, the occupants of the trucks with their hard suspensions would find themselves thrown from their seats; which is exactly what Tom was aiming for..

The trucks had been following a trail, but Tom was convinced that they would soon have to turn westward as he was sure that the spotter plane would have given them coordinates for where the herd was.

Looking at the map, Tom couldn't see anything that might act as a geographic funnel to get the trucks onto rocky terrain, but maybe from the air they could spot a few areas where the road narrowed enough to put in pressure pads.

'Damn it, they could take so many routes!' Mike cursed as the savannah opened up to wide between the rocky outcrops.

'Where does the depression start?' Mike was referring to the slight downward flow of land all the way to the Limpopo River. The trucks still had to go down a short landfall of around two metres onto the lower plateaux as they had chosen to follow the road that was on this small ridge.

'You're right, Mike. That's it! They will probably go down at the first opportunity. Get us in line with the ridge. Maybe we can gauge the route that that they're most likely to follow.'

'Okie, dokie.'

Mike flew low over the ridge and there it was, near the road, a dual track most probably used by Sally or some of the other rangers to go to the north-western watering holes. The dual track was one of the only ways to get down onto the plateaux without going over rocks and boulders.

'That's the spot! But we don't have much time. Mike, land quickly. Rusty, can we set the charges and then fly off and wait?'

'We can. But it would be better if we could set them off ourselves. More accuracy that way. The choice is yours.'

'What do you recommend?'

'To make sure the job is done right, I can perch behind some rocks over there.' Rusty pointed to a clump of trees about a hundred metres from the trucks. 'That would be fine from a distance perspective, but I'm not sure how I will get away once the tyres are blown.'

'Mike, any ideas?'

'I don't know. It's pretty flat here. Nowhere really to hide a chopper. Maybe we could fly east for a kilometre and land? We take off just before the trucks arrive and as Rusty sets off the charges, we fly in and pick him up behind that tree line. Should give us some cover and we can fly east away from the ridge '

'Sounds good. What do you think, Rusty? It is pretty dangerous.'

'Nothing I haven't handled before, Tom, The way I see it this is our only option, and we don't have any time to waste.'

'OK, Mike. Land and let's get this done.'

Mike landed the chopper a hundred metres away from the tracks so as not to leave any trace of their presence. Tom and Rusty ran to the tracks and laid out the charges – two packs in each spot about 20 metres apart. As back-up they did the same twenty metres on. They would probably only get one chance at stopping the trucks.

Rusty checked his equipment and gave Mike the thumbs up. At his signal, Mike took off and headed east.

Rusty and Tom busied themselves with covering up their tracks, which was easy given that the sand was so soft. Herds of animals had also been using the tracks for easy passage, so there were many tracks covering the ground. There was no way the truck drivers or their spotters could tell that Tom and Rusty had been there.

When they were satisfied, they ran to the clump of trees where they lay down on the ground behind the cover of the golden grass that grew around the clump.

'I hope there are no snakes.' Rusty poked the grass around him with a stick.

'They are long gone, Rust. Especially after all the noise you've made.' Tom smiled.

The bush was very quiet compared to the noise of the Huey. Surrounded only by the sounds of birds and insects, it was easy to hear the trucks well before they arrived.

'OK, mate, we need to make this work, otherwise we may end the day in a wooden box.' Tom grimaced.

'Don't try to cheer me up.'

The two friends had left stick markers to indicate where the explosives were.

'Here, Tom.' Rusty passed Tom the second set of remote controls.

'Push the red button twice to arm and once again to fire.'

Rusty settled himself with his charges, which were the front two. Tom would hopefully not need to do anything.

Less than half a kilometre away the trucks snaked their way around trees and rocks following the sand track. At the fork in the track, they stopped, and the commander shouted some orders to the truck behind.

The trucks started up again, and the lead truck took the left fork leading to Tom and Rusty's trap. The other one, however, drove straight on.

'What's he doing? '

If the second truck followed the track it was on, the soldiers in the back under the canvas canopy would be able to see Tom and Rusty as they were exposed from the side. They couldn't risk moving now though as the truck would drive right past them on the north-eastern track.

The first truck drove quickly through the sand and would be at the drop soon.

'Mike! Come in, Mike.'

'Hear you loud and clear, Tom.'

'We are in position, but the trucks have split. We'll hit the one as best we can, but the other may get away, please be in position for extraction.'

'Right-o, Tom. On my way,'

The trucks had slowed just short of the charges as the ground fell away down the track and the two tracks were positioned unevenly.

'Here we go,' Rusty said as he opened the remotes and quickly gave them a double click to arm before steadying his hands and thumbs in readiness to blow the charges.

The truck that had been crawling down the decline came to a halt just short of the charge. The commander was looking through his binoculars at the distant veld. Tom could see him pointing off into the distance, where you could clearly see a dusty cloud, most probably the herd, and they were not too far from here. The second truck had carried on driving and in a few seconds would be able to see Tom and Rusty lying in wait.

Rusty lay dead still, but Tom was restless and anxious.

As the second truck drove up towards the clump of trees where Tom and Rusty lay, it too came to a halt. Tom could see the commander in the first truck on the radio. They had spotted the herd and the other truck would not have to scour the ridge for a sighting. Reversing down the track, the second truck joined the first before they both began the descent.

The spacing of the charges was perfect. The lead truck's front tyres were directly over a pack of charges at the exact time the second truck's back tyres were over another.

Rusty clicked the remotes and the ground under each truck exploded, sending sand high into the air. Both trucks stopped. The front truck had a punctured front tyre, while the back vehicle's rear left tyre was on fire but was still inflated.

'Good job, Rusty.' Tom turned and smiled. 'Our luck is back.'

Tom and Rusty crawled backwards from the clump of trees and made their way across the ridge to where they could hear the Huey approaching. With a graceful swoop, Mike picked up his friends. As they took off they could see the black smoke from the rear vehicle and troops scattered in amongst the rocks, cautiously pointing their guns and scanning the bush for invisible enemies. A few soldiers shot at the helicopter, but from the distance there was little chance of a bullet doing any damage.

Mission accomplished.

'Woohoooo!' shouted Mike. 'That's one to the Green Team. Colonel zero.'

Tom and Rusty smiled, but Tom knew they were still a long way from safety.

13h58

Mamabe handed the Colonel the phone as they drove through open grassland.

'What is it?' the Colonel snapped.

'Sir, we have been ambushed!' The truck commander's voice came booming through the phone.

'What? How?'

'There were mines or something, blew out our tyres on both trucks. We need to be towed from the sand to get new tyres on.'

'You get those trucks out before we get there. I am very disappointed.'

'Mamabe,' the Colonel said, handing him the radio. ' Mamabe, today is not going well for us. First from Jonas, then the vet lady and now this.'

'Sir?'

'These people are just game rangers, who have they got with them that could blow off the truck tyres? Who is helping them?

It seems that they have constantly been one step ahead. And that helicopter, where does it come from?'

14h10

Sally had her hands full. Driving on the western side of the herd on a slight ridge, she could see the entire herd. The great grey animals were at a slow run, and Mopapi kept pulling them north. Even with three Land Rovers trained on trying to steer the matriarch, she still managed to turn the herd. Sally's concern was growing, as she had not heard from Tom or Mike for some time and the receivers showed no signal from their radios. They must have switched them off.

'We are going to have to get that chopper back.' Sally turned to Thabo.

'I will try them again.' Thabo picked up the handset. 'Green two to Goodair, come in please.'

All that came back was static.

Thabo repeated the call.

'Green two, this is Goodair. We hear you loud and clear.'

'Where have you guys been?' asked Thabo.

'Been trying to sabotage the Colonel's progress. Sorry about no contact, but we had to turn the radios off while we were busy with detonation devices. Rusty did a great job and the two recon trucks have been stopped, but we are not sure for how long. The Colonel is close behind, but we have laid out some obstacles for him. At least we hope so. How goes it with the herd?'

'Struggling, Tom. The big girl doesn't like taking orders. They are still moving, but not in the right direction. We need chopper assistance.'

'On the way. Will update you when we get back. See you in five.'

Sally smiled at Thabo.

'Looks like they've bought us some time. I think it's time for another break. Slow the team down and give the herd five minutes to catch their breath.'

14h45

The thick sand was getting the better of the Colonel's convoy. They had been brought to an almost standstill, and some of the older trucks needed to be towed.

As he sat in his Jeep, Moroge wondered why the world was against him. This was supposed to be a smooth operation. It was in a private game park, with nobody except staff around for miles. No soldiers. No anti-poaching units. So why were there helicopters and a team of some kind sabotaging this operation?

Moroge's convoy was driving along a sand track leading up a small ridge between two hills covered in large round boulders that had been worn by years of exposure to the sun, wind and rain. The convoy funnelled in, one behind the other, with the Colonel's Jeep just behind the leading truck. As they approached the narrowest point, gunfire shattered the drone of the convoy.

The Colonel was exposed in the back of the Jeep, but Mamabe was quick to order the driver to drive to the left of the lead truck, giving them cover from the gunfire. The Colonel could hear the bullets hitting the ground near him and he shouted for everyone to take cover. He was, after all, a seasoned soldier and as a soldier, in times of war, he had been a hero; a courageous man who led by example. Moroge felt the need to once again feel like a hero well up inside of him.

As the Jeep and the truck came to a halt and the convoy behind them pulled up to the side of the track, gunfire erupted from the other hill. The Colonel and his troops were exposed. Signalling for all to find cover, Mamabe leapt behind the large tyres of the lead truck and, lying flat on the ground, fired his rifle. As the troops leaped in behind the cover of the trucks they too opened fire into the boulders of the hills.

The Colonel, who had crawled under his Jeep, was also firing his automatic pistol into the boulders. Mamabe was shouting orders but his troops could not hear him. Every man with a gun was blasting an invisible enemy. With their first magazines spent, troops reloaded but shots kept coming from above.

'Mamabe!' the Colonel shouted. 'Can you see them?'

'No, Sir. We are exposed. We must try to break out.'

'Yes. They are on both sides and on the high ground. We need to move back.'

'Yes, Sir.'

'Is anyone hit'?

'No,Sir.'

And then it occurred to him. The Colonel had been in many skirmishes and firefights. There was always the sound of flack and bullets hitting the metal of vehicles. It was a sound he had grown used to. But now that sound was strangely absent. Perhaps the marksmen were too good, as there were bullets hitting the ground around them?

Once again there was a break in fire and all the soldiers reloaded in turn. In the break of fire, the volleys from the hills suddenly ceased.

'Cease fire!' Mamabe shouted.

'Mamabe, we must try to get up that hill. It may be that there are only a few of them, maybe even one on each hill. Split the teams and on my signal we must race up the hill, take them by surprise.'

Mamabe gave the necessary instructions, splitting the troops into two assault teams, one for each hill.

An eerie silence followed the gunfire.

'On my signal... Now!' shouted Mamabe.

The Colonel crawled out from under the Jeep and stood ready to run, but his age and girth had slowed him. His team was already halfway up the hill. Behind him, on the other hill, Mamabe and his team were already at the summit.

The troops ahead were nervously pointing their guns in all directions, but looked confused as to what they had found.

When the Colonel arrived at the top, out of breath, his troops walked up to him holding long threaded lines of spent charges.

'What is this?

'We are not sure, Sir. We found them behind those rocks.'

'Can you see anything else?'

'No, Sir. Not even tracks leading away. These must have been planted earlier. There are some tracks leading from the road up here.'

The Colonel looked across to the other hill. Signalling Mamabe, he saw one of the soldiers with the same thread of charges. It had been a diversion.

'Get your men to scout around and see if there are anymore of these in the rocks, and do it quickly. I want to move out in fifteen minutes.'

The Colonel walked down to the road again and signalled Mamabe to join him.

'Mamabe, what do you make of this?'

'It seems to be some sort of trick, Sir.'

'Yes, Mamabe. To slow us down. That helicopter must be involved. There are no tracks away from here, so they must have landed here and been lifted away again.'

Just then a soldier called Mamabe to show him the pressure pads and some of the small charge pipes that made the sand jump on the road.

'Sir!' Mamabe called the Colonel.

'This is what they have been using on the road. It seems we were fooled.'

The Colonel could feel his anger growing. It was becoming personal, a fight for his family, and these interfering people were standing between him and his new life; a life that he was becoming more desperate to attain.

'Mamabe, we must stop these people, they must be stopped at all costs. We must get moving and run as fast as we can to where they are.'

'Yes, Sir. We can move out immediately.'

'Leave six troopers here, just in case we are followed. Give them orders to prevent anyone from coming up this track. It may be that there are others coming from the road or from camps nearby. Is there not an anti-poaching unit somewhere close by?'

'Yes, Sir,' replied Mamabe. 'They usually patrol the southern border at this time of the week. Jonas gave very detailed information about their movements.'

'They may be on their way and they are probably armed.'

'Sir, they are probably too far away to pose a threat.'

'Very well, but we must be vigilant. Today has not gone as planned. There is a lot riding on this for you.'

Mamabe understood this as a warning. If you failed the Colonel, the repercussions were usually dire.

Mamabe saluted and began shouting orders to the rest of the truck commanders. Troops hopped aboard their trucks and engines roared to life as they started to pull out from between the two hills. As the trucks pulled away, two heavily armed soldiers sat waiting behind some of the boulders, just in case they were being followed.

The Colonel sat in his Jeep, wondering what other precautions he would have to take. And what he was going to have to do to ensure that there would be no witnesses.

15h15

As the Colonel was pulling away from the two hills, Tom and Mike were once again pushing Mopapi to her limits. With the return of the helicopter, the team had managed to turn the herd back towards the west, but the pace had slowed. The herd had been running at quite a pace since dawn and were now tiring. Sally had also boarded the Huey as she wanted to get a better idea of the stress levels in the herd, especially with regards to the smaller elephant.

'They don't look too bad.'She turned to Tom. 'Looks like they are just tired. I think it's because they are all together. Look over there; we call that little one Mosely. He is the youngest, a male.' Sally pointed to the tiny calf standing next to his mother. He was small enough to be able to stand between her legs.

'Isn't it amazing that he can keep up? But he must be getting very tired. If he's still going I'm sure the rest of the herd are alright. We need to keep them moving. We're only half an hour away from the water holes, and from there only a few miles to the border. Tom, I think we have a chance.'

'Yes, Sal, we're getting closer, but we are being hounded and we are still far from being home and dry.' Tom reached out and held Sally's hand just as Mike appeared.

'Tom, we have another problem.'

'What's up, Mike?'

'Fuel. We need to refuel and the bad news is there is only enough left at the camp for us to fly for another two hours.'

'Okay. Mike, I think it's best if I join the ground team. Sally and I can try to keep the herd moving. Do you have enough fuel to get Mopapi moving again? A few low passes should give her the idea.'

'Yup, have enough for another fifteen minutes or so.'

'After you refuel, fly past us and on to the border. We need to find a corridor through the Mopane and we are much further north than expected. Don't waste too much fuel, though. Once you have found a corridor, land somewhere nearby and give us the coordinates. We will push the herd through to you.'

'Will do.'

Mike brought the Huey down and landed a few hundred metres from where the one group of Land Rovers was waiting.

'Mike, fly safe, and if you have a chance, fly high on your way back to the camp and see if you can spot the Colonel. I hope we bought some time'.

Tom and Sally climbed out of the Huey after it touched down and, crouching, ran to the nearest Land Rover. Mike waited until his friends were well away from the blades of the helicopter before he took off again and swept back south.

Thabo was in the driver's seat of the Land Rover.

'You drive, Thabo. You know this place better than I do,' Sally said to Thabo.

'Mike should be able to get them moving again, you guys have made real progress,' said Thabo.

'Green one to Green Team and Goodair.' Tom spoke into the radio.

'Just wanted to give you all an update. A Colonel in the Zimbabwean army is currently pursuing us. As we all know, he is after the herd that we are chasing, but this Colonel is very close behind and, based on the fact that he opened fire on the helicopter we were flying in, we can assume that he is aware of us and what we are trying to do. He is going to try to stop us. He is with a number of troop carriers full of heavily armed soldiers. The trucks, I assume, are also intended for transporting the ivory. I realise that the danger as of this moment is exponentially higher than we had expected and as such all of our lives are in danger. If any of you wish to remove yourselves from this exercise, you have the opportunity to do so now. The best route for you would be to travel east along the ridge and back to one of the camps. Please sign in should you want to stay on. You all have a few minutes to make up your mind. Over!'

Almost immediately there was the first response on the radio.

'Goodair is in,' responded Mike. 'If we don't make a stand here, then nothing is worth fighting for.'

'Thanks, Mike.'

'Green two is in.'

'Thanks, Rusty,' Tom answered.

Behind Tom Thabo put a hand on both Sally and Tom's shoulders.

'You guys know I am in.'

'We do. buddy, but we did not want to speak for you.'

And one by one all of the ground crew signed in, in support of what they had set out to achieve, even though they were risking their lives doing so.

'We need to get through to the thick Mopane bush, set a target of the following position.' Tom read them the coordinates and they all entered them into their GPS devices.

"We have one final run and then we are home. Mike, are you reading me?'

'Loud and clear. I am coming in for my first pass. Are you ready?'

'Yes, we're ready. All teams, keep them moving towards the target.'

Mike flew low and,, hovering just to the east of the herd edged towards them. Dust flew up all around the chopper. Once again the action gave Mopapi a kick-start. At first she looked back towards the valley, flapping her ears, but then turned and started a slow run at the front of the herd. They followed. Mike kept up the pressure by following just behind the herd and one by one the ground vehicles moved into place. Once the herd had gathered together and were all moving at speed, Mike pulled back.

'They look like they are moving well, Mike. Go ahead and refuel. We'll stay on their heels.'

'Good job, see you in a bit.' Mike signed off.

As Mike gained altitude and looked back at the herd, he realised just how much dust had been thrown up by all the activity.

'I hope that we haven't given our position away,' he thought to himself. 'Too bad if we have, though. Only way to get them moving again.'

Almost immediately after Mike had gained some altitude, he could see the glint off the windscreens of the truck convoy. They were much closer than expected.

'Goodair to ground. Bad news! The convoy is close, just two kilometres south-east of your current position.'

Tom was astonished.

'Hi. Mike. We obviously didn't slow them down as much as we had hoped. How quickly are they moving?'

'Moving pretty quickly, Tom. They seem to be travelling towards you.'

'How long you reckon we've got, Mike?'

'If you don't speed up, they'll be with you in less than half an hour. But there is good news. You guys are closer than you think to the Mopane. Just over the next rise. If you can get in there, it may stop the trucks.'

'Maybe we will have to go in on foot?' wondered Tom.

In the distance Mike could also see the shimmering reflection of the Limpopo River.

'Your call, Tom I can't see a corridor or opening over there, but I can see the border. The river is not very far.'

'Thanks, Mike. We'l keep pushing. Get back as fast as you can.'

The crossing was not too far in the distance. They had moved the herd well, but with the Colonel in pursuit they were still far from making it.

Mike turned the chopper to the east and made for his fuel. The gauge was almost on empty when he landed close to the supplies.

15h30

The Colonel saw the dust cloud in the distance and ordered the convoy to stop. Looking through the binoculars he could see the helicopter hovering close to the ground.

'How far are we, Mamabe?'

'Not far, Sir. About two kilometres. We should be on them within the next fifteen minutes.'

'Tell your men to get ready. We are going to surround them and then kill them, elephant and man alike.'

The Colonel looked at Mamabe with resolute eyes. Mamabe knew it was not a good idea to argue, but these innocent people dying was not part of the brief. He paused, reluctant to order his men into action.

'They are not innocent. Mamabe. They are stealing what is ours, stealing our future. They are nothing. We must rid this country of them.'

'Yes, Sir.' Mamabe picked up a radio and gave the order to shoot to kill, telling the convoy to split up and surround the herd as well as anyone who was with them.

On the move once again, the Colonel's mind wandered back to a time where the enemy was evil and the fight was just. This time he knew that this was not the case, but he also knew that this was the best chance he had. Wiping his head with a handkerchief he waved on the convoy and then sat down before Mamabe pulled in behind the lead truck.

Not too far from the convoy, the Colonel could clearly see the dust lifted by the rotors of the helicopter.

'At last we are close to the goal, even if this herd has help,' he sighed, beginning to show some signs of fatigue. But this was not a time for rest. He went over in his mind what he needed to do.

'Get the ivory in and deliver it to the buyers later tonight, they should be waiting at the entry bridge to the south. My family should be waiting for me tomorrow at the airport and we can leave straight away, no waiting around. They will only miss me the following week as I have applied for leave and they think I am going to Johannesburg. I will explain myself to the family; this must be done as we are starting a new life. I hope they understand, but they have supported me blindly for so long anyway.' His thoughts trailed into the hot bushveld afternoon.

15h40

The sun was beginning to retreat into the west by the time the herd reached the Mopane belt that ran from north to south against the border of the reserve and through to the Limpopo River. The Mopane bush was thick, with small trees about three metres in height growing close together, creating a natural barrier for the Land Rovers which could not travel through unless a suitable path was found. The leaves of the trees were a thick mixture of browns and greens.

The herd, led by Mopapi, was only a few hundred metres from the Mopane bush. Under pressure from the Land Rovers, they were about to run down from a shoulder in the ridge. This gave them and the Land Rovers herding them a good view of the bush that lay ahead. The Mopane was thick all along the border, enjoying the depression that ran down to the river as protection against the heat. The extra moisture from morning dew and summer rain gave the trees enough moisture to thrive. Tom, Thabo and Sally's Land Rover was still the closest to Mopapi, who had kept the herd running.

'I cannot believe her. She made it possible for us to cover this incredible distance in such a short time. And she's injured,'

Tom pointed at her flanks. 'She's bleeding quite badly from that bullet wound. One tough girl.'

'The fact that she's injured makes me wonder even more what is going through her mind.' Sally leaned forward to get a better view.

'Guys,' Thabo interrupted, 'I have known Mopapi for many years now. She is wiser than you think. She has some sense of what we are trying to do.'

Thabo came to a stop on the side of the ridge as Mopapi kept on moving into the open plain towards the Mopane. In a trail of dust, her herd followed.

'Green Team, keep them moving, we are getting close,' Tom crowed into the radio. 'We need to see if anyone is behind us, Thabo, Can you get us to the top of that ridge?'

Once the herd had passed, Thabo drove a hundred metres or so up the ridge to a good vantage point and as the dust settled Tom could see the tracks they had created behind them. Two hundred plus elephants made quite an impact, especially when they were so close together.

As the dust settled further, Thabo noticed just below the ridge something kicking up some dust .

'Is that one of the herd?

'Shit no, that's them!' Sally shouted.

'Shit, they're right behind us!' Tom could see eight troop carriers travelling at speed about two hundred metres away.

'Drive Thabo, drive!' Tom yelled. They were now in plane sight of the troop carriers.

As Thabo turned the Land Rover they could hear shots being fired from below them and a shower of bullets hit the Land Rover. The front windscreen shattered. Thabo did not try to drive along the ridge, instead he shoved the Landrover into high range and revving, ploughed it down the ridge shoulder and onto the plain below. As they hit the flat ground, they heard the front drive shaft give under the force of the fall.

'Drive! Drive, Thabo!' shouted Tom. 'We need to get into the Mopane.'

Grabbing the radio, Tom shouted orders to the team.

'Everyone, the Colonel is right behind us and they just shot out our windscreen. Please, do not continue chasing the herd. Try to get those Landy's into the Mopane as fast as you can. Once the Colonel is on the ridge, we will all be exposed. Drive, everyone, drive. Unload what you can. Rusty, this would be a good time to let me know if you have any ideas.'

'Will do, Tom. There is one thing we could try, but we would have to get the herd into the Mopane. Then I might be able to create some cover for us if the wind is still in our favour.'

'Awesome. What's your idea, Rusty?'

'Make it into the trees and I will tell you.'

15h50

The Jeep carrying the Colonel, who was standing shouting orders, drove ahead of the trucks. The trucks were driving fast and kicking up dust and sand as they flew up the ridge.

'Mamabe, get them moving' The Colonel motioned to his men. We need to get to that herd before it gets into that thick bush. Shoot anything that moves, other than the herd. We need to keep them together.'

Mamabe was shouting orders into his radio set. 'Trucks one to four, go left. Trucks five to seven, go right. Try to encircle the herd; they cannot be far now'.

Soldiers in the back of each truck were busy loading up after their volley of shots at a single Land Rover they had seen on the ridge.

'Mamabe, when we get the herd down, make sure we start cutting the ivory immediately. I still want to make the deadline.'

The Colonel felt young again, in the throes of war. He could feel his heart racing and a wicked smile broadened across his face. He was enjoying himself.

15h50

Smoke started bellowing out of the engine. Thabo was driving as fast as the broken drive shaft would allow. As the Land Rovers pulled away from the herd and drove directly to the Mopane bush, the herd slowed and then stopped just short of the protection the bush had to offer. From the ridge, the Colonel and his troops would be able to take open shots at the herd; but, given they wanted the ivory, they would probably have to wait until the troop trucks had surrounded them.

The Land Rover's engine started screaming as they raced across the plain. They started to slow down. Most of the others had by now managed to get to the protection of the Mopane trees. Land Rovers were scattered all across the edge of the trees, but Tom, Sally and Thabo still had another hundred metres to go. Their engine gave one last scream and then exploded, oil and petrol igniting.

'Jump before the tanks blow!' Tom leapt from the burning vehicle closely followed by Thabo and Sally, who was covered in glass from the shattered window. They ran for cover, but the Land Rover exploded, sending glass and metal into the air. The blast knocked them to the ground. Thabo was hit by a flying sheet of metal that bruised his back and shoulder, and Sally had a few superficial cuts that were starting to bleed.

'We've got to move it. We're too far way from the trees!'

Tom grabbed Sally's arm and the three started to shuffle towards the protection of the bush where the others had gathered all their equipment together. Rusty was digging in one of his boxes when they heard the explosion.

'Tom, come in!' Rusty clicked on the radio.

There was no answer, just static.

'Tom, come in!'

Still no answer. Rusty and two others ran back to the edge of the thick bush where they could see the plumes of smoke pouring from a burning Land Rover. In the distance were three limping, shuffling bodies, but most shocking of all was the sight of a number of trucks driving down into the open plain. The herd had scattered northwards but were still in the open. Mopapi had stopped and was looking back at the trucks and the burning Land Rover.

'Damn it!' shouted Rusty. 'We need to do something and quick. Guys, come with me.' Rusty turned and ran back to a small clearing a short distance into the bush where they had dropped some of his boxes.

16h12

The Colonel was smiling. Before him he could see the herd, all mulling together. The day that had seemed to be against him now looked like it was bowing to his will. He could also see a burning Land Rover and, further beyond, the shapes of three people limping towards the Mopane belt. They still had fifty metres to go

'Fire at will, Mamabe!'

'Fire at will!' Mamabe shouted

The trucks had stopped behind the Colonel's Jeep and a few of the young soldiers had jumped down. They looked at Mamabe for confirmation; they were just young boys, drafted to assist with killing elephant, not people. The excitement of the hunt was now replaced by the reality of taking human life.

'Men, fire at those three people fleeing. They are the enemy!' the Colonel shouted.

Three of the soldiers pulled their rifles off their shoulders and took aim, but none of them fired.

'I said fire!' screamed the Colonel.

One of the men fired, but aimed too high, his bullets sailing over his targets' heads. Then the other two fired, but they were too far left. The wind had also changed and the smoke now hid the crouching figures.

'Mamabe, your crew is useless. Get me down there. I will take them out myself.' The Colonel pulled out his automatic pistol and loaded it.

'The rest of you, get moving, I want that ivory cut up and loaded before sunset. That gives you only two hours.'

Mamabe jumped into the Jeep and, moving rapidly down onto the plain, drove directly to where he thought the three people were hiding.

'They're shooting at us!' shouted Sally.

A bullet whistled passed them and hit the dirt just in front of them. Then another two shots, this time closer.

'Get down!' shouted Tom. They lay flat in the dirt. 'Holy shit.'

'Where are they firing from?' Thabo scrambled around in the dirt.

I cant see, there is too much smoke.' Tom looked around.

'Is there anywhere we can hide?'

'I can't see anything. We need to get to the bush.'

'Where is Mike? Tom! Is Mike alright?'

'I'm sure he's fine, Thabo. He's refuelling with a hand pump, so my guess is he's still pumping gas. We're all fine. But we are going to have to make a run for it. You guys ready?'

Thabo and Sally were a little stunned, but nodded their agreement.

'Okay, Tom.'

'Okay. We run across to that tree.' Tom pointed to a large dead tree amonst a group of smaller dead trees, the closest thing to protection from a hail of bullets.

'OK, let's go!'

Thabo, Tom and Sally started to run. They had only fifty metres to go. Tom turned to look back at the ridge, and saw a Jeep driving across the plain.

'Shit. Thabo, we're not going to make it.'

Thabo looked back. They could both see the Colonel in his green uniform, standing in the front of the Jeep with his gun in hand, coming for them. They could see that he wanted to kill them.

'Keep going!' Shouted Tom. 'We can make it. Just keep going!'

The Colonel waited until the Jeep was up close before taking aim. The soft sand was however making the Jeep bounce, and he couldn't get a shot in. Mamabe drove the Jeep right up to the three fugitives and as they drew up, the Colonel fired. A bullet whistled past Tom's ear.

Tom turned from Sally and Thabo and ran straight for the Jeep. Mamabe swerved away, thinking maybe the man was armed, and the Colonel lost his balance and fell from the Jeep into the sand.

'Sally, you carry on running. I have to help Tom.' Thabo turned and Sally scrambled up to a group of large tree trunks surrounded by thick bush.

The Colonel stood up, facing Tom, his back to the bush behind him. He was full of sand and had a gun in his hand. He held it in his right hand and pointed it at Tom, using his other hand to dust himself off. Just behind the Colonel, Mamabe was driving up in the Jeep.

'I have you now. Who are you, anyway? You are interfering with government business, a crime which will end in your death.'

'I know who you are and what you're trying to do,' answered Tom.

'Well it is none of your business. It is time you people left. But you will never see another day in Africa. This is your last.' The Colonel grinned. He was enjoying this adversary.

'You're not going to get away with this, Colonel,' shouted Tom. 'We'll catch up with you sooner or later,'

'How do you know I am a Colonel?' shouted the Colonel, surprised.

'We know all about you, Sir. Jonas was very informative.' Tom answered, gritting his teeth.

'Well I have had enough talking.' The Colonel lifted the gun.

The Colonel fired a single shot just before Thabo jumped on him from behind. Before Mamabe could get his gun from his holster and fire it, Thabo had wrestled the Colonel to the ground and, punching him three times in the face, rose from the dust with his gun. Mamabe fired, but missed at close range. Thabo turned and fired, and Mamabe fell to the sand with a single blood-red hole on his forehead.

Thabo ran to Tom, who was clutching his shoulder.

'Fucking bastard! He shot me!' Tom shouted.

'How bad is it?'

'I'm not sure. It hurts like hell.'

Almost in a haze, Tom's vision seemed to fade, but he realised that something was kicking up lots of dust.

'Mike's here.'

Thabo grabbed Tom and lifted him form the ground. Looking back, he saw that Sally had disappeared into the bush.

Mike brought the helicopter in close and Thabo supported Tom until they had made it to the door. Behind Thabo, the Colonel was stumbling to his feet and climbing back into the Jeep. Thabo turned to fire, but then chose to focus on Tom instead.

The sound of the helicopter drowned out all other sound, except that of the bullets hitting the windscreen. It was lucky for them that Mike had landed between them and the trucks, but the chopper was taking a beating.

'We have to get you to a Doctor, Tom. You're losing blood.'

Tom had been hit in the shoulder and blood was oozing from the wound, staining his shirt.

'I'm fine, just get us in the air. What about Sally though? Where is Sally?'

Everything was spinning out of control. They didn't have the time to wait for Sally. The chopper was already lifting off the ground.

'She'll be okay, Tom,' shouted Thabo over the noise of the chopper. 'She knows this area like the back of her hand. We'll come back for her.'

Tom, Mike and Thabo piled into the chopper and Mike lifted off. They flew in low over the herd and Mopapi, who had been watching once again, darted at the sight of the helicopter, this time deciding to make for the thick Mopane bush. Her herd, scattered by the gunfire, turned in behind her and followed into the bush.

The Huey was damaged and red warning lights were flashing on the dashboard.

'Come on, baby. Don't let me down.' Mike was silently coaxing the chopper westward over the thick Mopane bush.

'I can't keep her up very long, guys. We're going to have to land.'

Tom looked out and saw black smoke pouring from above them. The engine noise grew louder and then started to whine. Still being hit from behind by volleys of shots being fired from the ridge, the Huey suddenly dove to the left. Mike used all his skill to hold her nose up. Luckily they were only fifty feet over the thick bush.

'Were going down, hold on everyone!' Mike shouted above the noise of the engine.

Mike managed to hold her nose up just before impact. The Huey ploughed into the front edge of the Mopane. Branches shattered the cockpit glass and smashed into Mike's face and body. The Huey suddenly jumped up and spun ninety degrees as the rotors hit the trees and the ground. Tom and Thabo, who had strapped themselves in the back row of three seats, were thrown forward so hard that the nylon seatbelts cut into their shoulders. The Huey came to a standstill on its side, nose in the sand and tail caught up in the first line of Mopane trees that littered the southern side of the plain. Tom and Thabo were so winded they could not speak and writhed around in pain from the slicing action of the nylon belts. Mike's face was bleeding badly. A branch had slammed into his head, snapping on impact and leaving Mike unconscious.

Tom was the first to come around, his shoulder burning. Dark red blood stained his white shirt on both sides, one from a bullet, and the other from the seatbelt strap. His eyes were hazy from the impact. He looked outside the Huey and saw only blue sky above. Turning, he could see Thabo below him, moving slowly. The other door was just above the sand and Tom could see the red soil. Thabo started moving slowly, gritting his teeth.

'Thabo, are you okay?'

Thabo shook his head slowly, but said nothing.

'Thabo!' Tom leaned across to shake Thabo, but he could not lift his shoulder and a sharp spike of pain brought tears to his eyes.

Thabo continued to stir. The cabin was starting to fill with smoke and Tom could hear Mike coughing.

'Mike, are you alright?'

There was no answer.

The smoke grew thicker and Tom started to choke. Thabo too inhaled the grey air and started coughing. Tom tried to get the clip on his strap to open, but his hands could not move. The smoke was getting thicker.

'We have to get out!'

Thabo was mumbling now and looking around.

'Get out!' shouted Tom. 'I can smell fuel!'

Looking around, Tom could also see a grey liquid growing on the red soil.

'Can you get me out?' Tom shouted to Thabo. 'I can't move my arms.'

Thabo had regained his senses and caught hold of the webbing, balancing himself. He lifted his weight off the straps so that he could undo the clip. Climbing down he helped Tom lift his weight and undid his clip.

'Can you hold on to the webbing?' Thabo asked Tom.

'Yes, should be able to.'

Once the straps were off, feeling started to come back to Tom's good arm, but his shoulder was still bleeding badly. He grabbed the webbing and gripped it with his good hand. Thabo let Tom go and climbed across to the opening to the pilot's seating. Branches and leaves were in his way and he had to pull them away to get to Mike.

'Mike, are you ok?' Thabo pulled himself across and saw Mike's face, covered in blood.

'Can you move, Mike?'

Mike nodded, wiping blood from his eyes.

The smoke was getting very thick and Tom was finding it hard to breathe. Looking up, he could see blue sky through the smoke. He tried to push himself up on the webbing, which caused a sharp pain to erupt inside his shoulder.

'Is Mike, alright?' Tom shouted.

'He's going to make it. Just cut up a bit.'

'I need help. I can't get out on my own.'

Thabo looked back and could see Tom struggling to hold on to the webbing.

'Give me a moment. Mike's stuck in here. Can you hold on?'

'Yeah, I think so.' Tom swung around on his good arm, but could not use his other hand at all.

Thabo undid Mike's belt and pulled him up.

'Ahgghhgg!' Mike screamed as Thabo pulled him.

'I think it's my leg.'

Thabo looked down and saw that Mike's leg had been crushed.

'Looks like it's broken, Mike, but we have to move you. The smoke is getting thicker and there is fuel everywhere. Grit your teeth, brother.'

Thabo pulled Mike out of his seat and half carrying, half dragging him, shuffled up to where Tom was hanging on the webbing. Turning around, he helped Mike steady himself using the webbing.

'I will go up first and pull you guys up.'

Thabo climbed out of the side of the Huey and, leaning back through the opening, reached for Mike, who had good arms but a bad leg. Pulling hard with Mike pushing on his good leg, Thabo pulled him out.

'Your turn, Tom. Before you grab my arm, can you reach the Medikit?'

Tom opened the small box at the back seat and pulled out a small emergency medical kit bag. He passed the box to Thabo, who threw it to the ground.

Thabo again reached down and Tom grabbed hold. Mike also leaned over as Thabo pulled Tom up and grabbed Tom's bad arm.

'Agghh!' Tom screamed. The pain was unbearable as bone crunched against bone, but they got him out.

Below them, the fuel ignited. It would only be a few seconds before the fire reached the fuel tanks and exploded. Thabo pushed Mike backwards off the burning wreck and, holding Tom in front of him, jumped down onto the red sand. The three stood up and, holding Mike between them, Tom and Thabo hobbled away from the burning chopper. Not more than ten metres away, the helicopter exploded, sending wreckage flying into the air. The heat and blast threw the three men to the ground, wreckage spiralling above them.

Tom lay on the ground clutching his throbbing shoulder. His eyes were watering and his face was full of sand. He rolled on his side and looked up. He could not tell where he was. Mike was writhing around on the ground gritting his teeth. The blast had winded him as he had fallen on a rock. He could not even breathe and was gasping empty breaths. Thabo was the only one of the three who remained uninjured and he too was feeling battered after both the crash and the blast. Dragging himself up onto his knees, he looked around and saw that the three of them had run away from the bush and were once again in the open. In the distance Thabo could see the convoy of trucks driving towards them.

'We need to hurry!' Thabo's thoughts were muddled, as he was still trying to orient himself, but Tom and Mike needed help and he was going to have to take the lead. Looking back towards the burning Huey, he could see the bush burning. It seemed that the wind was blowing in a light southerly direction. If they could get behind those flames they would be safe.

'Tom, Mike!' Thabo grabbed their arms. Both grunted in pain, but heard his call.

'Come guys, we have to move. No matter how painful, we need to get back into that bush. Mike can you hold this?' Thabo passed him the medical kit.

Tom looked back and saw the flames growing in the dry trees that edged the plain.

Thabo stood up and, holding his friends' arms, he got them to their feet. Shuffling along, they covered the ground quickly and made for a small gap in the trees. They quickly disappeared into the bush and the smoke from the growing fire behind them. As they moved into the trees, the first of the trucks pulled up and out jumped a group of soldiers armed, with heavy machine guns. With orders being yelled by their commander, they ran into the bush behind Thabo, Tom and Mike.

Rusty had heard the helicopter come into land as he was dragging some of his boxes closer to the open plain. He had also heard all the gunfire that had ensued. The drone of the helicopter had suddenly replaced with a whine. He had looked up, but couldn't see anything through the thick Mopane trees. As he neared the edge of the trees, the ground opened up and he started to run. It was then that he heard the crash and the earth shook under his feet.

Sally had been hiding in the bush near the edge of the plain, crouching behind some old dead tree trunks. She had stood up when she heard the explosion and, running out from behind the tree trunks, she slammed into Rusty. They both fell to the ground.

'Sally, I thought you were with them?'

Shaken, Sally and Rusty hugged each other.

'What was that explosion, Rusty?' Sally had tears running down her face. This was not supposed to be how things turned out.

'It sounds like the chopper crashed. It must be nearby.' Rusty pointed to a plume of thick black smoke erupting about fifty metres away.

'They may be alive. We need to hurry!'

Rusty and Sally ran along the edge of the bush and could see yellow flames curling into the sky. Off to their left, through the trees, they could see the convoy approaching, three trucks all driving towards the downed Huey.

As they approached the site of the crash, they could feel the heat of the growing fire. The trucks were close and had stopped just short of the edge of the Mopani tree line. Shuffling through a thicker patch of trees, Sally saw movement ahead. At first she thought it was an animal, but then she saw the three shapes.

'It's them!' She pulled Rusty's shirt. 'I can see them!'

They broke through a thick group of small trees and there, on the ground, was Tom, Thabo and Mike.

'You guys are okay!'

Sally was crying and could hardly see through her tears. She went across to Tom and knelt down where he was lying, gently moving his head to her lap. She could see both Tom and Mike were in a lot of pain, and her relief that they were alive transformed into serious concern again.

'You're a sight for sore eyes.' Tom looked up from where he was lying.

'Quiet!' Rusty whispered, holding his hand out and standing very still. Through the leaves and branches, he could see figures moving. Sally and Thabo sat still, looking in the direction of Rusty's pointing hand. Sally was low to the ground and through a gap in the trees could see the booted feet of soldiers passing slowly southwards. She signalled Rusty that she could see them by pointing at her eyes and then making the same gesture in the direction of the soldiers.

Rusty mouthed words without making a sound. 'How many?'

Sally held up both hands with fingers extended.

'Shit, we need to get around them and back to the equipment,' Rusty said to himself.

Signalling Sally to stay put, Rusty touched Thabo on the shoulder and bent down to his ear.

'Buddy, I have an idea.'

'What's on your mind, Rust?'

'The wind is picking up, blowing west. The bush is dry. That fire is going to move across to us pretty quickly. All my kit is behind that fire. If we move almost due east as close to the fire as possible, we should be able to get behind the fire.'

Thabo nodded. 'If we can get everyone to the other side of the fire,' he whispered, 'we can light a line of fire behind us. Maybe those soldiers will follow the herd behind us and we can get free.'

Tom was listening, and even though he was wracked with pain, he signalled Sally to call them over. Sally waved at Rusty and Thabo, who moved close to her and Tom. Mike lay next to them, clutching his leg.

'Good idea, Rust, but we must try to get the herd behind the fire. Why not light a break downwind from us? Then we can move straight across to it.' Tom's face grimaced with pain as he spoke.

'Good idea, Boss, but that will also make us vulnerable. The soldiers will see us.'

'Perhaps. Not if there is a lot of smoke, though.' Tom smiled at Rusty.

'I'm with you,' smiled Rusty, 'I'll get back and create a screen for us. If I lay it close and the wind stays in behind us, we should have good cover.

'They've gone!' Sally whispered.

'Good, we need to move quickly.' Thabo stood up.

'It looks like the fire is spreading fast.' Tom was looking up. The smoke had thickened as the dry bush caught fire and columns of white smoke swirled above them.

'We'll need to move from here, but it's going to be slow. We will keep on our beacon so you can pick us up on your GPS.' Tom handed Rusty his GPS so that they could set them to track. 'Will you be able to get back to the kit and back in front of the fire in time to light a break, Rusty?' asked Tom.

'Yup, I believe we can. There is some open bush to our south. We can move through it quickly, but the fire will be there soon, so let's get going.'

'Great, you can see where we are on the GPS. We'll move south-east to the edge of the fire. If we can make it around, meet us there. If not, come and get us if you can.'

'Got you,' answered Rusty. 'Tom, if you have a problem light your own break.'

'Has anyone got something to light a fire with?' asked Sally.

Tom and Mike checked, but they had nothing.

'Rusty pulled a large paraffin lighter from his pocket and handed it to Sally. Always prepared.

'Rusty, I'll go with you. You're going to need some help.' Thabo looked at Tom to see if he approved and Tom smiled back.

'Cool, wish us luck.' Rusty stood up and ,grabbing his backpack, started creeping through the bush directly eastwards. Thabo followed.

They soon disappeared into the brown of the bush.

'How are you guys feeling?' Sally looked down at Tom and Mike.

'My leg is killing me,' Mike said, holding his knee. 'I think it's broken. I won't be too much help for the rest of this adventure.' He smiled up at Sally.

'What happened out there?' she asked.

'Delusions of grandeur!' Mike laughed.

Sally became aware once again that Tom and Mike were in a lot of pain. They all knew they were a long way from any hospitals or from anyone who could give them help.

'I guess I got us in over our heads this time?' Tom looked across to Mike.

'No, buddy. There are always risks. We know this.' He pulled out the medical kit from under him. 'I forgot about this in all the excitement.'

Sally breathed a sigh of relief at the sight of the Medikit. She quickly opened the box and found it contained more than she expected.

'Let's take a look at you first, Tom.' She pulled herself out from under his head and lay him on his back. Pealing off his shirt, she took out some swabs from the kit and cleaned his shoulder wound with antiseptic.

'Agghhh, that stings.' Tom cringed, clutching a small tree trunk with his good hand.

'I'm going to give it a clean. There is no exit wound, which means the bullet must have gone into your shoulder joint. That is good. There may be only a small amount of internal bleeding.'

Sally cleaned the wound as best she could and wrapped a bandage around Tom's shoulder.

'That should stop the bleeding, but we have to immobilise your arm and that's going to hurt bit.'

'Do what you must, Sal. I trust you,' Mike said, looking into her eyes.

'Okay, we need to get you up.' Sally held Toms' good hand and pulled him into a sitting position. Sally could see that every movement was painful.

'Tom, I am going to need to move your arm across your body so that your hand is on your opposite shoulder. Then I can strap it. It's going to be painful, but you should be a lot more mobile and the position will also help stem the bleeding and immobilise the arm.'

'Just do it. I can't move my arm. You will have to do it.'

Sally had unwound a bandage and cut some tape.

'Okay, Tom, grit your teeth.'

Sally took hold of Tom's arm just below the elbow and moved it steadily across his body until the affected hand was in position over the opposite arm's collarbone. Tom shut his eyes and cringed in pain as Sally moved his arm, but did not make a sound.

'All done. You okay, Tom?'

Tom opened his eyes and tears ran down his face. Sally strapped him up tightly using the bandage and the tape. When she had finished, she moved across to Mike.

'Aren't we a shocking lot?' joked Mike.,'I can't walk. Tom can walk, but he can't use his arm. Together I suppose we are almost a whole man.'

Sally gave Tom two painkillers from the medical kit, the best she could do for him at the moment.

16h48

The Colonel stood on a ridge, looking down at what lay below. His head was wet with sweat, but his eyes were clear and sharp. He felt he was once again at war and free from his bureaucratic office. It felt good. He had been close to danger and adrenaline was pumping in his veins again after so many years. He felt like he was fighting for freedom again, fighting for a cause that was wrapped in honour.

He could see the bush burning around where the helicopter had crashed. He had seen his adversaries escape from the crash, but had also seen his troops run into the bush behind them. In the plain below him, the remaining troop carriers had stopped at the edge of the bush where the elephant herd entered. The Colonel could also see the herd in amongst the trees, their grey backs sticking out from the lower bushes. They were directly south of where the chopper had crashed. He lifted his binoculars, but could not see any of his men through the smoke. The three troop transporters were stationary to the west of the burning Huey, but there were no men to be seen at the trucks. The Colonel walked back to the Jeep and jumped into the driver's seat. Starting the Jeep, he grabbed the radio and switched it on, pushing the transmit button.

'This is Moroge. All of you who can hear me: we must get down to the herd right away before they scatter into that forest. I want you all on foot. Do not shoot them when you see them. Keep them on the move. We must try to group them together at the river. The herd will be trapped. Go to it, men, your pay depends on it. Commander Lentswe, send me two of your men to ride with me in my Jeep.' The Colonel put the radio down. Behind him two men jumped from behind a truck and ran to the Jeep. Standing at attention next to the Jeep, they saluted.

'You men, get in behind me, and if you see any of those people trying to stop us, shoot them!' the Colonel barked.

'Yes, Sir!' The two men saluted again and then jumped in behind the Colonel.

Driving the Jeep back down onto the plain, the Colonel was followed by the four trucks that had remained on top of the ridge.

'Time to finish this,' the Colonel muttered. 'We are very close now.'

He looked down at his watch. It was late in the afternoon.They only had an hour to bring down the herd. Then the light would start to fade. They had to bring down all members of the herd before dark as they would be unable to chase down any strays in the dark. Once they had killed the herd, they could gather the ivory after dark and still make their deadline. The trucks all had spotlights.'

16h48

Rusty used his small hand-held GPS to find his boxes. Thabo had followed him through thick bush and their arms and faces were covered in small cuts from the thorn bushes and a thick soot from the smoke. They had managed to cover the ground quickly, even though the bush was thick.

'There they are!' shouted Rusty, pointing fifty metres away to the edge of a small clearing.

Thabo turned around and looked back towards the fire. It was spreading white smoke and spiralling in to the sky. This part of the Mopane bush was very dry and had not been in a fire for more than a decade. There was a lot of dead grass and wood that would ignite fast.

'We better move, Thabo!' Rusty shouted. 'We need to take those grey boxes and these blue bags.'

'Got them.' Thabo stacked three boxes.

'Sling these over your shoulder.' Rusty passed Thabo the blue bags.

'What's inside?'

'Flares. We can use them to shoot behind us, to help spread the fire.'

'Good idea.'

Thabo picked up the stacked boxes and Rusty finished packing his shoulder bag.

'Ready?' Rusty looked at Thabo.

'Ready.'

Rusty turned and ran back towards the fire, with Thabo following him. The wind was still blowing easterly and Rusty quickly set his GPS back to where Tom, Mike and Sally were hiding.

'I hope they are well on their way to this side of the fire. If not, they will get stuck,' Thabo shouted.

'What about the herd?' asked Rusty as they entered the thick bush again.

'They should be fine. they will hopefully move further south, away from the fire and from the Colonel. Who knows, this fire may actually help us.'

Rusty and Thabo ran into the thick bush towards the edge of the fire.

Tom, Mike and Sally were on the move. Mike had his arms over Tom and Sally's shoulders. Sally's job on Tom's bad arm had given him some relief and the bleeding had slowed. His face still showed the creases of pain, but he had a determined look in his eyes.

'We have to get back past the fire!' Tom pointed south-east. He had pulled out his GPS and opened his compass. The bush they were facing was thick and it was going to be slow going with Mike having to be dragged.

'Mike, this is going to hurt, but we have to get through. Try to take the weight off your leg by holding onto us. Hopefully the painkillers will kick in soon.'

'I'm fine, Tom. Drag me if you have to. Let's get to the other side of that fire, its spreading fast.'

The fire was getting closer. They could feel the heat and small particles of smoke were drifting through the air. Ahead of them, pillars of smoke rose into the air. Sally entered under the first branches and was followed by a tight-jawed Mike, who fell silent. Tom helped from behind. There was about a hundred and fifty metres to go and the fire was picking up speed. Sally found that it was faster if she turned backwards and pulled Mike along. The bush in front had low-hanging branches, but the ground below was sandy and clear. Sally crouched down and dragged Mike, who pushed with one leg.

'How are you doing, Mike?' Sally stopped and looked down at Mike's taught face.

'I am fine, keep going. Let's get this over with.'

Sally took hold of Mike again and they started moving under the trees. The fire was close enough for them to hear its crackle and roar as trees ignited and for the first time they started to feel the heat.

Sally kept them moving south-east on the line that Tom had chosen, stopping every fifteen or so metres to check their direction on her compass. They were making progress, but the bush was thick and the fire was closing.

'Tom, those flames are getting closer, we had better move south. If we get stuck, we are all going to burn.' Sally's voice was shaky.

'We'll be fine, Sal. We just have to get to the edge and upwind. These fires move fast but they follow the wind. Keep going. I will keep an eye out for the fire. If it gets tight, we can move south.'

Sally once again pulled at Mike, who pushed with his good leg. Silently the three friends moved under the trees. To their right a growing column of white smoke was growing, spreading across at least five hundred metres of bush. The ground was opening, but the fire was getting closer.

'Stop for a second, Sally.' Tom called for a halt. He stood silently, listening. Mike looked relieved. His face was wet and his jaw muscles had started to cramp.

'What is it, Tom?' asked Sally, who was breathing heavily from the exertion.

'I thought I could hear voices. Must be the sound of the fire. We must keep moving. Tom pointed forward and helped Sally pick up Mike who was lying on his back with his eyes shut.

The fire was spreading fast and was now pushing them sideways, the flames only twenty metres away. Although the bush had opened up, the wind had also picked up and they would have to run if they were to make it round and behind the flames. Tom could see that they were not going to make it and the wind had also turned slightly south.

'Guys, we're not going to make it. We are going to have to turn west. Shit!' Tom bent down onto his haunches and cradled his shoulder in his good hand. Looking up, he saw Sally's energy was almost spent and that Mike was close to passing out.

'Look, Tom!' Sally pointed just behind them. There was another fire, about fifty metres south.

'It must be Rusty.'

'Let's move. Last push! We need to get into the break. These trees are too close together and if we get stuck here we are going to fry.'

Sally and Tom pulled Mike through two more thickets. Mike was no longer helping and had started drifting in and out of consciousness. Sally was exhausted and fell to the ground. Tom too was exhausted and the blood he had lost was taking its toll. His strength was waning. As the three lay on the ground they could see above them that they were lying below two columns of smoke. The heat around them was growing and the loud cracks and whistles of the surrounding fires were getting louder.

Tom was about to pick up his radio, when out of the bush behind them came Rusty and Thabo, their faces covered in cuts from the bush.

'You guys are okay! We thought we lost you. The GPS was playing up, giving mixed signals. Must be the fire.' Rusty bent down next to Tom while Thabo checked on Mike, who was writhing around on the ground.

'We're not really okay, buddy. We're stuck.'

'Not really, matey,' answered Rusty. 'We have a way through, but we have to move fast.'

Rusty helped Thabo lift Mike onto his shoulder while Tom and Sally found their feet.

'Follow me!' shouted Rusty as he turned and moved west, directly towards the fire. Behind them the raging fire in the east was only fifteen metres away. Thabo was strong and carried Mike, who had now passed into a light coma, easily. Tom and Sally followed as best they could. Rusty covered the ground quickly and as they approached the fire, they could see a round opening between the Mopane trees that had already been burned by the backfire break. It was about thirty metres from side to side. Thabo carried Mike to the centre and put him down. Sally, Tom and Rusty surrounded Mike and, looking back, saw the fire raging just behind them.

'You lit this fire, Rust?' asked Tom?

'Yes, just in time, too. We were nearly caught behind the fire, but managed to make it round.'

'You did well, Rusty.'

They were all exhausted, sitting in a small huddle in the middle of a small opening in a Mopane forest surrounded on all sides by a raging fire. They sat as the fire grew to the edge of the opening and raged around them. The heat was unbearable, but not enough to burn them. Smoke poured in around them. Luckily the fire to the west of them had moved off. The smoke was being blown by the growing wind. Surprisingly, the swirling wind allowed them to breathe. Almost as quickly as it surrounded them, so too did the fire die and an opening of breathable air gave them relief.

'We have to move again,' shouted Thabo. 'Towards the river, otherwise we might be seen. We need to get across the river.'

Tom lay on his stomach. He was covered in black soot and tears from the smoke had left trails down his cheeks. The rest were the same. Mike was still coughing, but they all had survived. Thabo lifted Mike carefully with Rusty's help and then began to move southwards into the smoke and soot of the fire's aftermath.

17h00

The Colonel had moved all his troops into a line on the western side of the fire. The troop carriers had also driven westward and found an opening into the thick Mopane, but it hadn't gotten them very far. The herd had moved further towards the river, but the Colonel knew that he had the manpower to kill them all before the sun was down. He pulled out his radio for one last instruction.

'Men, this is Colonel Moroge. Listen carefully. You are all in position and must make your way directly south. There must be no shooting until I give the signal. We must surround the herd and then kill them all in one sweep. The elephant are only a few hundred metres away. They are just on the other side of the fire. Move carefully and only take your rifles, no other kit. Keep silent until I give the signal. If you ignore my orders, I will shoot you myself. Now move!'

To the left and right, the Colonel could see his troops being instructed by their crew commanders. Across the line they all threw down extra kit and made their way into the first line of Mopane trees.

17h15

The five friends bundled closely together and moved south towards the river. They passed through some of the thicker burned bush, but the southern side opened up into savannah leading down to the river. Rocks and boulders were scattered amongst the grassland.

Rusty was weighed down with the weight of his shoulder bag. Thabo too was carrying two heavy bags and shared the weight of Mike, who was still drifting in and out of consciousness.

'Are you ok, Sally?' Thabo could see that she was shaking under Mike's weight.

'I'm fine! Tired!' Sally pulled on Mike's arm to secure his weight over her shoulders.

Tom moved slightly ahead, looking for the herd.

'I can't see any of them!' he shouted. 'Maybe it's too late.'

'Here, have a look through these.' Rusty passed Tom a small pair of binoculars.

The sun had just started setting in the west and the sky was starting to light up with the bright reds and blues. The smoke had also emphasised how clear the sky beyond it was.

Tom wiped the binoculars and scanned the bush slowly. Looking to the river, Tom scanned westwards. The sun made it difficult to see and Tom's eyes were full of dust and soot. He rubbed them and then had another look.

'I can't see them.'

'Tom!' Thabo called.

Tom turned and saw Thabo pointing due south towards the river, more or less a kilometre away. At first he thought they were big grey boulders, but then he realised they were moving. Tom pulled the binoculars to his eyes again, his good arm shaking.

'You're right! It's them! They made it round the fire to the river!' Tom's voice echoed his relief. 'We need to get to them, fast. We need to cross over. The Colonel and his men can't be very far away.'

'You're right, Tom, but we are weighed down,' replied Sally. 'Why don't you, Thabo and Rusty go? You can get them moving again, and there is something between you and Mopapi.' Sally touched Tom on his shoulder.

'You guys wait here then, we will try and get them across.'

'Marcus should be somewhere over the river with the collection team. We must try and make contact. Maybe he can help. They are not very well armed, but they may be able to give some of the Colonel's men a scare.'

'Good idea,' replied Rusty, handing Sally the GPS. 'Yyou guys settle in here and try to make contact. The Colonel can't be far. The fire may have pushed them back, but I'm sure they will be onto us soon.'

Thabo carried Mike to a rock and lay him with his back against it. Mike's eyes were closed.

'Mike must have passed out. How is he doing, Sally?' asked Thabo.

'Pulse is fast, but he is doing fine. I think the pain and exhaustion was just too much,' answered Sally.

Thabo smiled at Sally, who lay next to Mike, and joined Tom and Rusty as they made their way towards the herd.

Over a small rise a hundred metres away from where Sally and Mike had settled, the three had a better view of the herd and they stopped to get a better idea of how many there were.

'Guys, there are a lot of them. Fortunately, they are all together. Must have been drinking. Looks like some of them are wet.' Tom looked back at Rusty and Thabo. Both were smiling with tears in their eyes.

'Fucking hell, I can't believe they are okay.' Rusty crouched down on his haunches.

'I wonder how many there are? Have you spotted our girl?' Rusty asked.

'There she is, on our side. Mopapi, good girl, you managed to take them past the fire.' Tom spoke with great emotion. This elephant was definitely getting under his skin.

'Well it has been a hell of a day, but we still need to get them home. We are close, but there's no cigar until we are on the other side.' Thabo spoke with a sigh of relief.

While the three friends watched the herd from the small rise, the sound of an engine suddenly echoed off the rocks around them. Turning to look west, Tom could see the Colonel's jeep driving slowly through the rocks. It was no more than a few hundred metres from the river, just west of the herd. Behind the jeep, running out of the smoke, was a line of troops, around twenty of them, all running. They were making their way directly towards the herd.

Tom knew that the only way they could stop them was to kill them.

'For fuck's sake, does this guy never give up?'

Tom was exhausted, but he stood up and took a deep breath, turning to Rusty and Thabo. Without another word the three started running towards the herd. If they were quick they would be able to get between them and the Colonel. Tom wasn't sure what they could do when they got there, but as they ran Rusty pulled some canisters from his bags. While running, he pulled out pins from them one at a time and threw them to the ground. Each one erupted with green or orange smoke. As they ran, Tom could see that the wind was blowing the smoke towards the Colonel.

'Great idea, Rust. Pass us a few of those!' Thabo shouted.

Rusty passed out what he had as they jogged towards the river.

'Thabo, when you are finished with these, get the flares out. We can try and scare the herd across with them. These explode thirty seconds after firing. Lots of fire and noise, but not very dangerous. They certainly won't kill anyone. Might scare the shit out of them though.'

Rusty and Thabo managed to throw down more than ten canisters as they covered the first hundred metres to the river.

Tom was running as fast as he could, but his shoulder was burning again and he could feel wet, warm blood running from his shoulder again. He was losing ground on Thabo and Rusty. Looking towards the Jeep, Tom could see the Colonel standing in his seat, waving towards the smoke.

'They've seen us!' shouted Rusty. 'We'd better move it!'

The wind was swirling the smoke around them as they ran. They were halfway to the river when both Thabo and Rusty shot off the flares in the direction of the herd. The red fiery orbs drifted out towards the herd and, just after hitting the ground short of the herd, they exploded. The herd reacted quickly, running away from the noise towards the water, but the river was wide and deep. The herd stopped. They were spread across a good two hundred metres of shoreline, in some places ten elephants deep. Tom could see that they too were exhausted, standing still and looking at what was chasing them.

Still running quite far behind Thabo and Rusty, Tom could see Mopapi emerge from amongst the herd, facing the direction where the flares had exploded.

'Run, girl, run!' Tom shouted. He was still too far away for it to have any impact. Looking to his right he could see the Colonel and his troops breaking out of the rocks onto the bank of the river. The herd was wide open and seemingly dazed by all that had happened. If they didn't move, this would be the end.

'Thabo, Rusty, shoot at the Colonel!' Tom gave out a cry and then his feet gave under him as he fell down into the sandy earth. The pain in his shoulder tore through him and he winced and groaned. Struggling to his knees, he looked on, only to see Rusty and Thabo leaping behind a small clump of rocks. Tom could feel his exhaustion, right to his bones, but he rose to his feet and carried on moving. He could feel his vision blurring a little and his breathing was too fast, leaving him heaving for air. He found himself stopping short of the eastern shore side of the herd. Around him he could hear bullets ricocheting off the rocks and in the distance small bursts of fire from a row of soldiers. Standing facing them he could see that it was too late for the herd. They were stuck between the river and the Colonel. To the west the fire was burning down towards the water, covering the shore with thick smoke, and to the east there was a flow of orange and green smoke from the flares Thabo and Rusty had fired at them. To the north was the colonel with twenty trigger-happy soldiers, firing their rifles at will. Nowhere to run or hide.

Mopapi stood her ground. looking towards the Colonel and his men, who were now within firing range. Tom could hear the Colonel shouting orders and saw the soldiers turn their fire onto the herd. Everything went into slow motion. He could see Rusty and Thabo firing flares at the Colonel, but none of them found their mark. Behind them, he could see the herd standing, looking, not moving, waiting for Mopapi to decide. He had never seen a herd so unable to react.

'Run!' Tom shouted as loud as he could, but the wind, exploding flares and the clatter of gunfire muffled his cry. At first the herd seemed to stay still, but some of the elephants at the front were being hit by a shower of bullets. Mopapi threw her head high in the air and gave off a scream that filled the air. The soldiers stopped firing, but the Colonel ordered them to move forward towards the herd. Then Mopapi charged. She took aim at the Colonel and raced towards him, covering the ground between rapidly. The soldiers seeing her in full flight turned and ran. This time, though, she was not alone. Fifteen of the herd had joined her. She bowed her head low as she ran, flapping her ears, and through the smoke Tom saw some of the soldiers turning and firing at her.

'She won't make it,' Tom whispered to himself, before falling to his knees.

Mopapi raced towards her enemy, enraged once more. She had had enough. No more running. She honed in on the men. Her senses focused on the threat. Behind her ran the others, also taking fire but closing in fast. The Colonel took evasive action in the Jeep and drove towards Tom. Tom could see Mopapi's chest redden. She was taking the most damage, but she had moved so fast that she was close to the first group of soldiers. They were too slow to move and she slammed into them, knocking bodies in every direction. Behind her the other herd members trampled the soldiers one by one, lifting red dust into the smokey air. Broken bodies were speared to the ground by large tusks.

Mopapi didn't stop. She ran down the second group who tried to scatter but the other herd members gathered close to Mopapi and they obliterated each and every soldier. Tom could not believe his eyes.

Mopapi turned towards the Colonel's Jeep. The Colonel was close to Tom, but had not seen him. Standing, Tom pulled out the flare gun that Thabo had given him, aimed it at the Colonel and fired. The flare ignited and flew low to the ground, hit the front of the Jeep and exploded. Flames bellowed out from the front of the Jeep and spread into the engine. The Colonel jumped from the vehicle just before it burst into flames and ran towards Tom.

Tom turned to see where Rusty and Thabo were and saw them shooting flares at the herd, which by this time had withdrawn into the river up to their waists. They were too far away to hear Tom shouting and the Colonel was too close. Tom stared at the Colonel who ran up to him, rifle in hand.

'You bastard!' the Colonel shouted. 'You have ruined this day for me and for that you shall die.'

The Colonel slammed the butt of the rifle into Tom's stomach and he fell to the ground. Tom heaved and writhed, winded, exhausted, swirling in a mist of pain and emotion. The Colonel grabbed him by the hair and, turning him over, shoved the rifle barrel into Tom's mouth.

'Now you die, you bastard. You have killed me and my family, now I will kill you and yours.' The Colonel's eyes were glaring. Tom could see no mercy, only hatred and fear.

Tom could see the Colonel pulling back on the trigger when a huge white tusk shot out from the Colonel's chest. The Colonel's eyes widened, showing their whites, and Tom's leg was trampled by a heavy foot before he was thrown back against a large black rock.

The Colonel had been impaled by Mopapi's right tusk. It had gone through his back and out through his chest, and while she ran he was suspended in the air like a puppet, arms dangling at his sides. Mopapi shook him until her tusk tore free. He fell to the ground, where she trampled him until there was nothing more than a large wet, red stain on the dry earth. Tom lay only a few metres from the remains of the Colonel, but couldn't move. Mopapi turned and looked at him. He was winded and his leg felt like it was shattered. He could see her clearly, her eyes wild and her chest and legs wet with bright red blood. Tom could feel the vibration of more herd members running towards them. Tom knew he was next. The herd was enraged. His only thoughts were that they had succeeded and that he had never been so close to such a magnificent creature and that they were free. It was over.

As the herd approached, Mopapi gave a long deep call and they all came to a halt. Tom was surrounded by the largest members of the herd and Mopapi looked down at him on the ground for a few seconds before turning and slowly making her way back towards the river. The others stood for a few seconds, looking down at the Colonel's remains, before they too followed Mopapi to the river.

Tom looked out towards the herd through blurred eyes. Some had made it across the river. Thabo and Rusty were in amongst some thick bush on the side of the river, looking back to where he lay.

Looking back towards the solders lying on the ground, Tom could see three elephants lying on the ground. One was still moving, but the others were dead. Tom wondered why there was so little honour in man yet so much in these ancient beasts. His eyes were stinging, but he could not take his gaze away from the majestic Mopapi. Just then she fell to the ground and emitted a deep droning call that filled his eyes with tears. The call was answered and the larger herd members that had fought alongside her all surrounded her and touched her where she lay. Tom's eyes closed and he drifted off into swirling oblivion.

Chapter 10

09h35, Tuesday 18 September – Polokwane MediClinic, Northern Province, South Africa

Tom woke and through blurred eyes saw the smiling face of Sally sitting on the bed beside him.

'Welcome back.' Sally gave Tom a broad smile and reached down to hold his hand.

Tom tried to sit up, but a sharp pain tore through his chest and shoulder.

'Hey, relax Conan. You've been shot and your leg was badly mauled. I recommend you lie back and rest.'

Tom lay back, grimacing with pain.

'How long have I been out?'

'Long enough. They removed the bullet, but you were really lucky, Tom. It didn't even break the bone. How are you feeling?'

'A bit groggy. It's good to see you though. I thought it was all over.'

'Not at all, Tom. You did everything you could, and more.'

Sally bent down and gave Tom a warm kiss on the cheek. She smelled of fresh soap and shampoo, and her long hair tickled his cheek.

'Hey, I like the nurses in this hospital,' Tom smiled.

'For sure, but only for special patients,' smiled Sally.

'How are our friends?'

'Almost all of them are alive, thanks to you.' Sally smiled but a tear welled up in her eyes.

Tom remembered that Mopapi had fallen.

'She's gone?'

'Yes, she saved all of us and almost the entire herd. I had a look at her when we passed and she had taken at least fifty shots to the chest. She was strong, very strong, but not strong enough for that.'

'How many others fell?'

Sally was wiping her eyes. 'Nine altogether, and we are having to treat a few of them. There were a lot of bullets, it was a mess.'

'I'm sorry, Sally. What happened after I passed out?' Tom tried to pull himself up again.

'Hold on, Champ, let me wind the bed up.' Sally helped hoist the top of the bed to bring Tom upright.

'Well, Marcus was not too far away. Actually, he saw most of it from the other side of the river. He had some of the South African border patrol with him, some vets and a few army officials. They were amazing. They helped to get the herd together and built an enclosure. They managed to get us all across the river. If they hadn't been there, I think we may have lost you.'

'What about our support teams? What happened to them when the fire broke out?'

'You told them to get over the border, which they did. They missed all the action, but they're okay.'

'So where is the herd now?'

'They are camped up at Hein's place. We'll be moving them tomorrow. The trucks have all arrived, probably one of the biggest convoys in history. We should have them in their new home by the end of the week, and it looks like we have enough space to keep them all together.'

'Where will they be going, Sal?'

'A place called Itaga, a large private reserve. It's partly owned by some local government officials, which helped in keeping red tape to a minimum. They were very happy to help out and the reserve has ample land to support the herd. An enclosure for them has just been fenced and it seems like the vegetation in the area is pretty overgrown and just right for their diet, so it's looking pretty good.'

'Is the reserve kosher?'

'Yes, as far as I know. It's basically private, mostly for government visitors. I am sure there will be some hunting, which we can't stop, but it's really more for travelling dignitaries who want to witness the jewels of Africa. The herd should be safe there for a while.'

'That's great news, Sally.'

Tom looked into Sally's deep blue eyes and smiled warmly as he squeezed her hand.

'So what are you up to then? What's going to happen to Chikangawa?'

'I'm not sure, but the press in South Africa has had a field day with this. It was in yesterday's paper. Apparently the Colonel was in deep trouble and owed money, lots of it.'

'What a lunatic.'

'Seems he was stealing money from the wrong people, namely his own party. His family had their picture in the paper. They were arrested at the airport trying to board a private jet on its way to England.'

'We were lucky, Sally. It could have worked out far worse than it did … for all of us. Just a few wrong turns and we would be the ones six feet under.'

'I know, Tom, but I can't help thinking that what goes around comes around. The Colonel got what he deserved.'

There was a knock at the door, and Mike's face appeared from around the corner.

'Hi there, war heroes, ready for a visitor?' Mike gave his friends a broad grin.

'Hey, Mr Mike. How goes the mercenary pilot?' Tom was very happy to see his friend was up and about.

Mike came through the door on two wooden crutches, his leg in plaster up to the knee.

'That looks good on you my friend.'

'I look good in anything, even plaster.'

Sally got up from the bed and gave Mike a big hug and a kiss.

'I am here as a messenger,' Mike said as he pulled a mobile phone from his pocket. 'Speak to your father.'

Mike passed Tom the telephone.

'Pop?' Tom held the phone to his ear.

'Son! I am so relieved that you are alright. How are you feeling?'

'Much better, but it was a close call.'

'Sounds about as close a call as it has ever been, Son. I wish I was twenty years younger so that I could have been there. How is the herd?'

'Sally says they are doing well.'

'Well I hate to bother you, but we have another job.'

'We do?' answered Tom, a note of excitement in his voice.

'Yes, it seems that those bastard seal-pelt ships are moving out of Japan again and your help is required in sinking the problem, so to speak.'

'When do we start?'

'As soon as you're up on your feet and can get back here. In the meantime, start giving some thought to getting a team together. Do you have any ideas off-hand?'

'Yes, some,' replied Tom, smiling at Sally and Mike.

'Okay, well for now just focus on getting well soon. And remember, I am very proud of you. I can't tell how relieved I am that you're all okay. I love you, Son.'

'Thanks Pop, I love you too. I'll give you a call in a day or so to confirm flights.'

'Excellent. Tell Sally I say hello.'

'Will do. Cheers, Pop.'

Tom handed Mike the phone.

'Guys, it seems as though we are needed elsewhere.'

'Well, I need a new job since some friend got me into this mess and I lost my contract with the Arabs,' Mike said as he lightly punched Tom on the shoulder.

'Ouch!' Tom yelped as he grabbed his shoulder in mock pain.

They all laughed as each of them wondered what adventure awaited them next.